BLURB

What could be worse than catching your creepy boss in an inappropriate position? *Hearing him say your name.*

Bailey

This day couldn't get any worse.

I just saw my boss Mr. Dent's extremely unimpressive... dent. A night of drinking with my best friend is exactly what I need. Hunter is always there for me. The perfect Mr. Nice Guy.

Hunter

This day couldn't get any better.

Finally I get my chance to show my best friend that I'm also the best guy for her. I just saw Bailey's perfect curves soaped up in the shower and all my dreams are coming true. Until she won't return my calls the next day.

Bailey wants to pretend none of it happened but I just need one chance to prove our attraction is real. I'm finally going to show her that I'm not that...nice.

WICKED

M. MALONE
NANA MALONE

ALSO BY M. MALONE & NANA MALONE

- The Shameless Trilogy -

Shame (prequel)

Shameless / Shameful / UnAshamed

- The Force Duet -

Forcful (prequel)

Force / Enforce

- The Deep Duet -

In Deep (prequel)

Deep / Deeper

- The Sin Duet -

Beyond Sin (prequel)

Sin / Sinful

1

———

Hunter

I heard her laugh first.

I was at happy hour, as usual, with some people from work, when across the room, I heard that laugh. Not just a feminine giggle, but a full-blown belly laugh. Me, and several other men in the bar, all craned our necks to see where it was coming from.

The thing was, it wasn't some melodic feminine laugh. Oh no. It was a full-on whole body guffaw. Not at all ladylike, but incredibly visceral. It made my lips twitch, her good humor contagious. It made me want to be near someone who could laugh like that.

When I caught sight of her, my heart tripped. Like I'd heard about in books. She was sitting in a corner with some people, a brunette and two other men. They looked about the same age. Maybe college. Maybe grad school. Probably around twenty-three. Honey blonde hair, styled in big puffy curls, hanging softly down her shoulders. One of the guys said something and she laughed again.

Oh shit. I liked her. She clearly wasn't taking herself too seriously, like half the women here. Sure, she was wearing business casual, some kind of dress that wrapped around. It had flowers on it. I couldn't see her feet, but I assumed there was some kind of either, fuck-me heel, or chunky contraption. Sensible. For work. The brunette said something again. And then they all laughed.

One of my co-workers said something to me and I didn't even hear it. My gaze was still focused on the blonde in the corner.

I gave a haphazard answer and hoped it was the right one, but I couldn't turn away from her. Somebody must have alerted her, because suddenly, her head whipped around and our gazes collided. Instead of giving me the coy, slide-away-look thing, her gaze just pinned to mine. And then she did the most remarkable thing, she full on smiled at me.

That's all it took. Dick, hard.

I was so screwed.

Finally, my co-worker Mike saw what I was staring at. "Oh, so that's why you're not paying attention."

"Do you have any idea who she is?" I asked.

"Nope. I've never seen her here before."

Mike was married, so he could appreciate the view, but he wasn't any competition. At least not today. She turned back to her friends, and my brain went through all the scenarios in which I could approach her. I couldn't just walk up to her and start chatting her up with her friends right there. Odds were slim that would work in my favor. But no way I was losing the chance.

I was so busy running through all my scenarios and the best angles, I didn't even notice that one of her friends got up and left. Two minutes later, someone tapped me on the shoulder. When I turned, my heart did that stopping thing again. Which, could be danger-ous. I know.

The blonde stood right behind me with that smile again. "Hi. I'm Bailey."

"Uh, hi. Hunter Richards."

"Do you mind if I sit here? I'm waiting for someone to hand this off to. I don't want to occupy a whole table all by myself."

I stared at her, dumbfounded. *Yeah, smooth. Real smooth slick.*

Only when Mike nudged me did I manage to stutter. "Y-yeah, of course. Have a seat."

She grinned that sweet smile and then ordered a club soda.

"A club soda? At least let me get you a real drink."

I was relieved that my social cues kicked in. I was terrified that something about this girl had short-circuited my brain. Women had never been a problem for me. Usually, all it took was a smile, a flirtatious comment. I knew what I looked like. It helped that I was tall, clearly hit the gym regularly and that I was friendly.

She turned to me. "Okay let's have it. Favorite Star Wars character?"

I blinked for a second again. Why was she getting me so off kilter? "Excuse me?"

She pointed at my watch. I had the Star Wars face on my apple watch. "Oh, sorry. I forgot I was wearing that. I mean, Luke Skywalker, of course. I think he's every kid's favorite."

She shook her head. "Nope. I love Jar Jar Binks. He was funny."

My jaw unhinged. "Please, do not ever say that out loud. Do not ever, in public again."

Cue the laughing. I felt like someone had shoved a lightning bolt straight up my dick, and it lit up my whole body making every nerve tingle. She held on to the edge of the bar as she leaned back, her hair cascading in a honey blonde waterfall behind her.

"Oh my God. You should see your face. That's the best." Her head fell back again as she gripped her ribs and laughed even harder. "Of course, my favorite is not Jar Jar Binks. Oh my God, he almost ruined the franchise for me. I'm all about Yoda."

"I think I'm in love."

She winked at me. "Nah, you only think my choice of characters is cool. Imagine if it *had* been Jar Jar. That would have been the end of a glorious bar relationship."

I grinned back at her. "You know, I have been known to get over some bad choices. Just as long as you tell me you also love Star Trek, I would have gotten over it."

She narrowed her gaze at me. "Original, Next Generation or Voyager?"

I choked. "My God, Next Generation. Please don't tell me you liked Voyager."

She shrugged. "Honestly, I kind of liked Voyager. It didn't have the gravitas of Next Generation, but you know, it was still solid."

"Oh my God, you're killing me."

"What? A girl can't have a lady boner for Voyager?"

Then it was my turn to laugh. "Fuck, did you just say lady boner?"

Her grin was so wide and her eyes danced and

sparkled and in that moment I suddenly understood how these things happened. How people fall in love with just a look. I was so captivated by this girl I had completely forgotten about my friend who was sitting directly on the other side of me.

"I feel like I have to reprogram your entire binge watching situation here. Please tell me that you actually watch *cool* sci fi shit."

She shrugged. "I do like Warehouse 13. And I've totally binged Quantum Leap on Netflix."

I sighed. "I don't know what to do with you."

She grinned. "You know, you are not the first person who has said that to me."

And it went like that. I don't know how much time went by, just that the person she was waiting for never showed. We sat there chatting and laughing long after my friend tapped me on the shoulder and waved good-bye. It was like the best first date, that wasn't even a date, I'd ever been on.

Finally, she glanced at her watch and groaned. "Oh my God, I need to get home. I start my new internship tomorrow. I can't be out all night."

I glanced at my watch. "It's only nine."

"You got me. I have a ten-year old's bed time. I'm useless if I stay up too late. Besides, it's my first day. I want to make a good impression. You know, I have to obsess about what outfit I'm going to wear for several hours and agonize over my hair, only to end up looking just like this."

My gaze swept over her. "I don't know. You look pretty good to me."

A flush crept up her neck and then dusted her cheeks with a pretty pink. "Thank you."

Come on dude. Get your shit together. Get the digits. "So listen, we should definitely do this again because like I said, you need a lot of sci-fi deprogramming. So why don't you put your number in my phone?"

She grinned then, took my phone enthusiastically and then dug around her purse. "Mine is here somewhere. Hold on." She put her purse in my lap as she dug through it.

Did she have no idea what she was doing to me? How beautiful she was? But it was clear she wasn't being coy and brushing against me on purpose. No games. She was unabashedly herself.

She finally plucked out her phone and handed it to me. "Give me yours, too."

I put myself in as *Hot Hunter*. You know, that way she would always remember who I was. When she returned my phone to me, I saw that she'd just put in Bailey Jones. I adjusted it to *Beautiful Bailey* with the name of the bar behind it, so I would know who she was.

Because yes, I'm a bad boy.

She grabbed the folder she'd been holding on to and then hopped to her feet. "Well, it was very nice to meet you, Hunter. You should definitely call, or text, because really, who makes phone calls now? Who wants to talk with their voice, when they can just text out a message?"

She had me laughing at that. "That's a good point. But I don't know, I like your voice. Mostly, I like how you laugh."

Ahh, cue the pink flushing again. So pretty.

"Okay, well, I'm going to go, have a good night."

"Oh hey wait, what job are you starting tomorrow?"

She pointed down the street towards my building. "Bold Horizons. I start tomorrow. I'm so excited."

My face froze immediately. And she frowned. "What's wrong?"

"That's where I work."

Her smile deepened. "Oh fantastic. Then at least, I'll have one friend there."

I swallowed hard. "Yeah, you have one friend for sure."

———

BACK AT HOME, I tossed my keys onto the side table next to the door. That was one hell of a night. A night that ended with a boner Bailey would *not* be helping me out with.

Ever.

She was amazing and funny, and just my type of girl. But this wasn't going to happen. Just my luck.

At the thought of her, my dick twitched.

"Yeah buddy, I know. She was awesome. But we can't have her. No sex with co-workers remember? Bad idea."

My dick twitched again. That was basically the only response he was capable of at the moment.

I needed to do something about him, otherwise, it was going to be a long night. Maybe if I grabbed a shower and took care of the situation, then I'd be able to think clearly and I wouldn't have a single-minded focus on Bailey.

I'd be seeing her every day at Bold Horizons. No way in hell was popping a boner every time she walked by going to work out. She was awesome, and she thought we were going to be friends, so I would have to figure my shit out.

I started peeling clothes off as I headed towards the shower, my plan firm in my mind. A mindless orgasm concluded with crashing in bed. That's all I needed.

A trail of clothes marked my path. I'd pick them up on the way back. I wasn't a total slob, despite what my cleaning lady probably thought.

I grabbed a pair of boxers and a T-shirt from my dresser and headed for the shower. My watch beeped. It was an alert that a work message I'd been waiting on all day had finally come through. So instead of the shower, I diverted to my laptop first.

I tossed it on the bed and opened it up, determined to reply quickly, then get my shower and hit the sack. Thoughts of the shower conjured an image of Bailey wet and soaped up. My dick seemed to like that idea as it swelled even more.

God, I had it so bad.

The real question was whether being her friend was going to make it better or make it worse? I replied to the email and then frowned when I saw a deposit notice from my bank. I opened the email quickly and my brows furrowed. What the hell?

$9,999 had been deposited into my account.

It was a direct transfer. I didn't recognize the bank, or the name of the sender. BS Trust & Holdings. The name alone made me suspicious.

I had my own researcher on retainer. I liked to call him *Google*. I pulled up a search window and typed in BS Trust & Holdings. My eyes scanned the search results, not that there was much to see. It appeared to be a local import-export based right here in New York City but not much else was available.

Awesome.

I made decent money. Hell, *good* money. But a sudden influx of almost ten grand was still nothing to sneeze at.

There was a time when that would have been a life-changing amount of money. I grew up in foster care in Long Island. Some places had been really great. My last place was outstanding.

My foster dad was the professor at a college. He figured out how to teach me so that shit was interesting. I got into a good college, thanks to him. Some of the others before him, had been not so good. Those places had been borderline abusive.

If it hadn't been for one of my foster brothers, Steven, I would have gotten my ass kicked daily. I always wondered what happened to him. I tried once or twice to find him, to see how he turned out, see if I could help him in some way, return the favor. But after I got transferred out of that hellhole, the word was he ran away. No one had ever heard from him again. I dreaded to think of what had happened to him after I'd been shipped out.

I stared at the amount of money again. In the morning, I'd call the bank. It might be a mistake. An incorrect account number, it could be anything. Or it could be something insane.

But insane things didn't happen to me. I lived a

perfectly normal life. Sure, I went out with a lot of women. No harm in that. On weekends, I liked to play. Hiking, sky diving, rock climbing... adventurous, yes. But there was nothing about my life to warrant interest from anybody sinister.

So who the hell put $9,999 into your account?

It was such an oddly specific amount. Another search yielded the very interesting fact that any deposit of ten thousand dollars or higher had to be reported to the IRS. And I was pretty damn sure that whoever made this transfer was well aware of that rule.

Which led me to wonder just what the hell was going on.

I had no idea, but I was going to find out.

2

Bailey

"So, tell me everything. How's the new job?"

I grinned as Talia prattled on a mile a minute. I was so excited we were going to be roommates next year when she transferred. "It's great actually. I *love* my job. And I'm learning so much. I mean, it was totally the right move."

"Oh good. Tell me if you start working on anything cool, like a marketing campaign featuring hot male models."

"If they let me near any hot models, you'll be the first one to know. But I don't think this is that type of internship. It's been a month and so far it's just admin stuff."

"So, who is your boss? Is he cute?"

"Mr. Dent? No way. My life is not a romance novel. I swear. If my boss was hot, that would actually be a problem. I don't want anything to mess up this opportunity for me. I love the job and I've already made some friends, so everything is really great."

"Oh cool. I didn't know if anyone would be weird because you're still in college. You know how they treat interns at some places."

"I was worried about that, too. But everyone has been so nice and really generous with their time."

"So now, you're not giving me any juicy gossip? Nothing at all? Ugh, it's so frustrating. I figured one of us would at least have something cool on the horizon, you know? Now you make me think of work as boring."

"Well, it's not boring. I just, you know. I'm not focused on guys." *Except, you do think about Hunter.*

As soon as that thought flowed, I shoved it down immediately. I was not going to think about Hunter. You know, anymore. Because I spent an embarrassing amount of time thinking about him. It wasn't intentional. It just happened. Every time I turned around, he was there. Being sweet. God, he was so good looking. The first night we met, I would have sworn he was boyfriend material. We just clicked like we'd known each other for years. Then I found out he worked here at Bold Horizons.

And that ruined that.

Sometimes I considered saying to hell with the rules, but I was an intern. Chasing after another employee was not a good look.

So, I would keep my head down and keep it professional, even if sometimes I did check out his ass. I mean, honestly, it would be a crime not to. But it wasn't like he was going to go anywhere. It wasn't like I could do anything about it.

The look on his face when he found out I worked here, was like someone had kicked his puppy. And I'd felt it, too. Which made no sense. It wasn't as if I knew him well. But just the idea that someone that hot was paying attention to me, and someone to share the fun dirty things that I did, that had been a total bonus.

But, it wasn't to be. So we had turned into best friends instead. Which was great. Awesome. I depended on Hunter. Honestly, I've learned so much from him already. He had been a life saver ever since my first day of work.

When Dent was driving me crazy, it was almost always Hunter who could calm me down and remind me of the benefits of working with a seasoned professional like Dent. Honestly, he'd become extremely important to my happiness here.

It's because you have the hots for him.

Okay yeah, I totally had a crush on him. It's kind of embarrassing actually. I spent an insane amount of time being preoccupied with what he was doing and when I was going to see him again.

It had to stop. I knew it had to stop. There was no way in hell I could ever tell him how I felt. It would ruin everything. He took his job here seriously. And I did, too. It didn't matter how good his ass looked in those dark wash jeans.

"No guys. I wish."

"Ugh! Total bummer, but you know what? When I get there, it's going to be awesome. School is going to be a blast. I can't wait for a fresh start with my bestie, ready for my new life."

"You betcha! I can't wait to have you here either."

I hung up with her, and saw that I'd had two texts come in.

Hunter: Shoot, Shag, Marry, Tyrion Lannister, King of the Dead, or Little Finger?

I smiled, unable to contain my grin. I replied immediately.

Me: I can't even do this. The dead guy is, well,

dead, so eww! Little Finger also eww! I do think Tyrion is deliciously dirty though.

Hunter sent back an eye roll emoji, and I chuckled as I got undressed for bed. Now all I had to do was remind myself that he was my friend. Those little thoughts I harbored about him, would ruin everything. So eyes on the prize.

Hunter, wasn't on the menu.

Hunter

It had gotten to the point that I knew exactly where Bailey was in the room without even having to turn to look at her. I could feel the energy vibrating between us. The moment she walked into the conference room, my gaze snapped to hers and I gave her a broad grin.

Yes, like a sap, I'd saved her a seat. *You have it so bad.*

Yeah I did. I had since I'd met her. But, what was that saying about shitting where you eat? I sure as hell wasn't going to do that. Except, I wanted to be the kind of guy who didn't bow to the rules. I wanted to be the guy who could just say fuck it, and take the risk. We could be adults, right?

It didn't have to be some big drama. The two of us could handle it. We could be total adults about it.

Who was I kidding? I wanted her. When she knew it, things would be awkward. Awful. Impossible. There would be no way to maintain our friendship. It didn't stop me from wanting her though.

Maybe this was the time to shoot my shot. Hell, I was feeling lucky. After my conversation with the bank, the one in which they'd assured me the deposit in my account was legitimate, I was feeling very lucky.

Someone had known I needed that money and had gone to great lengths to make sure I was taken care of. Obviously I was doing something right. Even if I still had no clue who'd sent it.

They'd gathered half the company inside of the conference room. Even though Bailey was clearly making a beeline for me, she kept her gait casual, as if she was in no hurry.

As if I wasn't dying from wanting to be next to her. From wanting to breathe her in.

Clearly you are the only one feeling this way. Pull your shit together.

"Hey." She said exuberantly.

I longed to take her, pick her up, and cuddle her tight. *Yeah, just like a friend.*

"Hey yourself."

"Do you know what this is about?"

"I don't know. All they told us was new policies. So that's all I got."

She nodded. "Okay. You all right?"

Had she possibly noticed that I was holding my breath, trying hard not to breathe in her scent?

"Yeah, I'm fine." The lies fell smoothly off my tongue. Because I was the kind of guy who wouldn't lie to his best friend.

The president of the company, Phil Lawrence, came on the screen. "Hello everyone, thank you for taking the time out of your day to join me for this meeting... "

He went on and on about the strength of the company, how he cared about every single one of us, how he regarded us as a family. Then he paused and I suddenly had the distinct feeling that this was no ordinary briefing.

"In light of recent sexual harassment complaints and concerns, we will be employing some new policies."

I sat up straighter. Complaints? What the hell? Had someone noticed me staring at Bailey's ass? Was that what this was about?

Don't be a dumbass.

My first irrational reaction aside, I knew that I'd spent more time keeping my eyes off Bailey than on, so it was unlikely that anyone else would have noticed it.

Phil continued. "There will be a strict, no fraternization policy between subordinates and superiors. So that means, anyone on the executive level, shall not carry on a relationship with anyone subordinate to them. There will be no exceptions."

Oh hell, there it was, all laid out in black and white. I was a junior executive. Bailey was an intern. I could only swallow, and any hope of actually having her as mine vanished without a trace.

"Special concessions will be made for prior relationship status. But by and large, this will be the new company policy."

Ugh, how was this even possible?

But he wasn't done. As he went on and on, it became clear that some idiot had abused his power and made someone else feel uncomfortable. So, thereby ruining it for all of us.

Bailey leaned over. "Do you know who he's talking about specifically?"

I shook my head. "No, honestly, it could be anybody. Half these guys are pervs." *Yourself included.*

She slapped my arm. "Be serious. You have no clue?"

I shook my head. "I mean, okay truth, marketing girls seem to be young and very pretty, so I have no doubt in my mind that some idiot thought he could get away with abusing his power. I just don't know who it could be. Half the guys here are married. Not that that would stop anyone. But I honestly have no idea who it is."

"This is going to get complicated. So many people meet at work. I'm not sure how this is going to go down."

I bit my tongue. "Dating someone you work with is tricky even if you're not a douchebag."

She nodded. "Yeah. It's what happens when you break up. Things always get ugly."

I nodded. She was right of course. But I just knew that for us, it would be worth it. But before I could open my mouth again, Phil Lawrence continued. "Any and all new relationships, will be violating the policy. Any attempt to circumvent the policy, will be met with strong punishment."

Would I be the only one punished? If it was just me that might get in trouble, hell, saying something might be worth the risk. But if Bailey could get in trouble, then no, I could be her friend. I could be good old Hunter. Even if it hurt.

"Well, I'm glad we have each other to lean on. I'd be completely lost here without you," Bailey whispered.

I could tell she meant it. "I feel the same way, kiddo."

Kiddo? Oh yeah, real smooth.

What was wrong with me? But she was right. In such a short time, she'd become one of my closest friends. Maybe that was better than having her as a girlfriend.

Who are you kidding? Having her for even one night would be better than not having her at all.

Well, as true as that might be, it was never going to happen. So I'd better let that go.

And figure out how to treat her like my friend.

3

————

Bailey

One year later...

I smiled to myself as yet another text came through.

Hunter: Get your ass down here now

It was Friday night and the rest of the office had already knocked off to go down to Happy's, the bar right down the street from our building. It was our favorite spot for happy hour, thanks to the cheap drinks and terrible music. I'd be right there with them if I hadn't gotten so behind on my work today.

Or if my asshole boss hadn't dumped project busy

work on me just a few hours ago. I wasn't even assigned to any of these projects specifically. Who did that?

Hunter: Charles from Legal is on the bar dancing. I think he's trying to twerk.

I snorted at the mental image of the older man trying to shake his ass. Our firm was a pretty conservative place and when I'd first started interning here, I'd been really intimidated. Everyone seemed so busy and professional, like they all had their shit together, while I was just trying to figure out what I wanted to do after college. But this was my second summer interning with the company and after a few Friday nights hanging out with the office crew, I'd discovered that even the most conservative types had a wild side.

Not that I wanted to picture the nice older man who always helped me with legal questions trying to gyrate his nonexistent ass. I giggled at just the thought.

Hunter: Seriously, where the hell are you?

Fed up, I finally responded. Damn, he could be such a drama king sometimes.

Me: Trying to finish all this work Mr. D gave me at the last minute. I could finish faster if you'd stop texting me!

I returned to my computer screen and squinted at the small column of numbers. I sighed. Numbers weren't my thing. I'd thought I was safe by majoring in marketing, but apparently even marketing majors needed to know how to adhere to a budget for their projects. My boss, Mr. Dent, didn't really seem to understand the budget all that well himself, though. Probably why he'd dumped this on me at the last minute.

After making a few minor changes to the numbers I'd entered earlier, I saved the file to the project drive and printed. It wasn't perfect, but it was the best I could do. What the hell could he really expect at the last minute on a Friday? It was already eight o'clock, and no one else had stayed this late. If I was lucky, Mr. Dent had fallen asleep at his desk again, and I could just slide this into his inbox without having to interact with him.

I hated having to talk to my creepy older boss, a man who still thought a comb over was preferable to just being bald, especially when there was no one else there to act as a buffer. It wasn't any one thing he'd done that made me uncomfortable; there was just something about the way he looked at me. I shuddered as I gathered my things. He looked at me like he wished he could see through my clothes. I sighed, realizing his cringeworthy gazes were the only action I'd seen in months.

I walked down the hallway toward Mr. Dent's corner office. My handbag thumped against my thigh as I walked awkwardly, trying to type a text to Hunter at the same time. Maybe if I hadn't been distracted, I would have heard the noises before I got to the doorway.

"Oh yes, that's it. Suck that dick."

I halted in the doorway, the hand that was holding my phone going up to cover my mouth. My brain was in such shock that I tried to cover my mouth and my eyes simultaneously, but I couldn't block the grotesque image playing out right in front of me.

The light was off in the room but Mr. Dent had a large picture window right behind him and the late evening light was more than enough to illuminate what he was doing. He'd pushed his chair back from his desk and sat with his legs spread, creating more room for him as his meaty hand tugged at the short, stubby penis protruding from his pants.

I clutched my phone tighter, my mouth opening and closing in shock. I knew I should probably move, but what if he saw me from the corner of his eye? So far, he hadn't noticed me, and I definitely didn't want to do anything to draw his attention.

"Oh fuck yeah. That's it. Yes. Yes. Bailey!" He shouted my name and let out a long, agonizing groan.

His hand moved so fast it was a blur, but there was no missing the stream of white that sprayed everywhere as he continued to groan out my name.

My name.

Horrified, I backed out of the room slowly. Luckily, Mr. Dent still had his eyes squeezed closed as his hand continued to pump absently at his now deflated mini-sausage. There was an expression of complete and total satisfaction on his face.

OhmyGodOhmyGodOhmyGod.

My heart was practically beating out of my chest as I trotted down the hallway, my phone still clutched in my hand. What the hell was that? Had he actually said my name?

I squeezed my eyes shut as a wave of revulsion swept through me. The elevator was right in front of me, but I was scared to hit the button. What if he heard me? Then I thought, *Fuck it*, and hit the button to call the elevator. If he hadn't heard me running down the hallway, then I was probably safe.

The entire walk over to Happy's, I replayed the last five minutes. It felt like a nightmare I couldn't wake up from. This was my boss! I had to go back to work on Monday and look him in the eye like nothing had happened! I almost gagged just thinking about all the times he'd come up behind me at my desk and put his hand on my shoulder.

For the rest of eternity, I'd have a new image of exactly where his hands had been. *Shudder.*

Hunter texted me again. Without even reading his message, I typed back.

Me: I am traumatized. There better be a drink waiting for me when I get there.

Suddenly the phone in my hand rang. I answered with a shaky "Hello?"

"What the hell happened? Do I need to kick someone's ass?" Hunter growled.

I clutched my bag tighter as I sped up. The front door of the bar was now visible. "It's so much worse than that. I'm almost there. And Hunter?"

"Yeah, baby girl?"

"I was serious about that drink. In fact, make it two."

———

Hunter

The things I did for the friend that I'd been crushing on for what felt like forever…

It was hard to believe that we'd only known each other a year. She'd started interning at my company the prior summer. There was a slight age difference—she was still in college, after all. But I didn't think that twenty-six was too old. There were advantages in dating a guy who was a little older. Advantages like the ability to not come in the first five minutes of sex and knowing what the clitoris was capable of.

I had mastered both in college and was a much better man for it. If only Bailey would let me show her. But she didn't see me that way. I was the charming guy who worked a floor above hers and was always up for a coffee run, not the one she wanted to drag into the supply closet and make out with.

As soon as Bailey appeared in the doorway of the bar, I could tell something was seriously wrong. She obviously hadn't been exaggerating when she said she was traumatized. Her eyes darted around the room wildly, like she'd just seen a ghost, and her hands shook as she tried to straighten her hair. That was another clue. Bailey always looked perfect. I'd never seen her with a hair out of place, but the bun she always wore was falling down and her hair hung loosely around her neck. When she saw me, her eyes lit up, which made me feel about ten feet tall.

Bailey pushed her way through the crowd and dropped into the chair across from me. Tables were always at a premium, so there were several other people I didn't know at the other end of the table. Bailey snatched one of the vodka shots from in front of me and tossed it back. I watched in amazement as she winced and then blew out a breath. Then she reached over and took the other one, the one I'd been saving for myself, and drank that too.

"What the hell happened to you?" I finally asked.

"Oh God. I don't even know where to start." She dropped her head into her hand.

I'd seen that she texted me some random video earlier, but I hadn't had a chance to watch it because her other texts had come rushing in. Knowing Bailey, she'd probably sent me another blurry video as she walked around the office. I'd never met a person worse with technology than Bailey. She also managed to butt-dial me frequently.

Finally she leaned closer. "You can't tell anyone this. I'm serious."

I pantomimed locking my lips with a key. "I'm a vault. Come on, Bay, you know I'm not a gossip."

She leaned even closer. "I saw Mr. Dent jerking off in his office." She took a really deep breath. "And then when he... you know, *finished*... he said my name. *Several* times."

After a long moment spent staring at her, I stood and went over to the bar and held up two fingers. A few minutes later I returned to the table with two more vodka shots. I sat down and slid one across the table to Bailey, who took it gratefully. She tilted her head back, and I watched her throat work as she swallowed.

Heat climbed my face. Damn, I was just as bad as her boss. Mr. Dent wasn't my manager, but he was the one who managed the intern program. He was a crotchety older man, the type who liked to argue just to hear the sound of his own voice. The thought of that dude wanking and fantasizing about Bailey was enough to turn my stomach, so I could only imagine how she felt. I took my own shot, hoping the alcohol could clear the image.

"Shit, you weren't kidding when you said it was traumatizing."

"Yes! Oh my God, how the hell am I supposed to go to work on Monday?" Bailey's loud screech drew some attention from the strangers at the end of their table. She shrank under their stares, lowering her voice. "And now I'm acting like the drunk crazy girl in the bar. This is just great."

Her words slurred slightly and I figured that was a sign. Bailey was a petite thing, so three vodka shots in close succession probably wasn't the best idea. But if any situation could benefit from a little alcohol-induced memory loss, this one qualified for sure.

"Come on, let's get you home." I pulled up the taxi app on my phone and called for a car. It showed one two streets away. I stood and held out my hand to Bailey.

She stood. "You don't have to do that. I appreciate

you listening. I didn't mean to make you leave early." She hugged me, wrapping her arms around my waist and resting her head right over my heart.

I tried to pull back slightly so she wouldn't feel the erection that was steadily growing. She'd just seen the grossest thing imaginable, so I figured the last thing she'd want would be to come into contact with dick of any kind. But when I tried to step back, her arms tightened and she pressed her face against my shirt.

"You're such a good friend!" she wailed. Since her face was turned into my chest, it came out muffled, sounding more like "Yooof such a goob fiend!"

I sighed. "Okay, this is not going to work. Come on, baby girl." I led her to the door, walking sideways half the time since she didn't want to let go of my waist. By the time we made it through the crowd and got to the cab waiting at the curb, Bailey was barely walking on her own and her hands had decided to take a walking tour of my body. I managed to get her in the cab, ignoring the skeptical look of the driver.

"Man, is she okay? She'd better not throw up in my cab."

I shot the guy a look. "Drive fast then." I gave him Bailey's address and then jumped when I felt her hand in my lap.

I gritted my teeth as I tried to peel her fingers off my thigh.

This was typical luck for me. The girl who'd never been interested in me before was handsy when she was drunk.

Typical luck.

4

Bailey

Once Hunter had me back home, I had an even more difficult time keeping my hands to myself. *Now wait just a minute. Hunter had all this going on?* I slid my hands over his pecs and abs, silently counting the muscles. Well, well. Hunter had been holding out on me.

Okay, I wasn't an idiot: he was clearly cute. Smoking hot, from a truly objective standpoint. He had dark brown hair that I was pretty sure he styled into messy disarray. His moss green eyes were kind and intelligent, but also really expressive. I could always tell his mood by his eyes. When I'd started at Bold Horizons, a year ago, my focus had been on my future.

What I did here would also get me into the MBA program.

So I'd worked hard to put thoughts of the super nice, super hot young executive out of my mind. Well, except when I was in bed, alone, with a vibrator guaranteed to make me scream.

I didn't have the best luck with guys, and I wasn't looking to make a mistake where I worked. I always chose wrong. And when it came down to it, Hunter had turned out to be a really good friend. When stuff at school was hard, I could escape into our friendship. During the school year, I commuted from campus, but since it was summer, the company had found me this corporate apartment as part of the internship program.

And now, I was here...with Hunter...and he felt so good. No, seriously, why hadn't I jumped his bones before? *Because you know how you are. Once you get close, you panic and you run.*

I knew this line of thought was entirely due to the copious amount of alcohol I'd imbibed. But there was a part of me that wanted to do this. This was *Hunter*. He was my friend. He was so sweet. Exactly the kind of guy that every girl should want to be with.

He took care of me, and did all the gentlemanly things you only read about in books. Even though we were just friends, every time he dropped me off at my apartment, he made it a point to walk me to the door and make sure I got in okay.

If he invited me somewhere, he insisted on paying. It all evened out in the end because I'd often bought the beers, but it was more than that. He listened. And whenever he had a girlfriend issue, he talked about each girl with respect. I'd never let myself admit it before, but I was always a little bit jealous.

Not because of the girls per se, because I wasn't looking for that from Hunter. *Are you sure about that?* But because of the kind of guy he was. I wanted someone like that for myself, eventually. You know, after I graduated and had my career on track. Then it would be time to find someone who wouldn't hurt me.

Except with Hunter tonight, with him holding me, I wanted him to help me forget. Forget what I'd seen and heard. *Ugh.* Please God, I really needed to forget what I'd heard.

And the more I touched Hunter, the more my brain focused on the tingling low in my belly than it did on the horrors I'd seen before I left the office.

"Hunter, how come you've never asked me out before?"

I could hear the question coming out of my mouth. It was like my brain wasn't in control. At least not the rational part of my brain, the part that would remind me that this was *Hunter*. He was my *friend*, and not some guy that I could just anonymously sleep with and walk away from.

Hunter cleared his throat. "Well, *Bay*, because we're friends. And you've always made it pretty clear that you aren't looking to date."

"And what if I've changed my mind?" I leaned into him. "What if I think I was being an idiot? What if I *want* you to ask me out?"

I lifted my gaze to his, and his pupils dilated as his eyes dropped to my lips for a moment.

Yes. The idea of Hunter kissing me made my clit throb. I pressed closer. God, he smelled amazing. And to think about him wrapping his arms around me as he kissed me and touched me and...okay, yeah, this Hunter thing, it seemed like a pretty good idea.

I stood on tiptoes, looping my arms around his neck. "You're my best friend. You take such good care of me. I especially need that right now. You want to take care of what I need, Hunter?"

My breasts pressed into his chest and my nipples hardened. Just being close to him and rubbing up against him lit my body on fire.

Oh, God, yes.

I licked my bottom lip, before pressing my mouth to his. For a moment, his hands tightened on my hips and he groaned low. The jolt of lust ran straight from my nipples down between my thighs.

But then something was wrong. Instead of pulling me closer so I could feel the length of him pulsing against my belly, he was pushing me...away.

"Hunter?"

He squeezed his eyes shut and clenched his jaw. "Bailey. Let's get you into bed. Pull out your pajamas or whatever and get changed. We can talk about this later. When you're sober. Because when you're sober, I am so down for having this conversation. But not now when you're trashed. Come on, off to bed."

I let him lead me down the hall to the bedroom, even as I muttered, "I like the idea of off to bed."

He chuckled low. "Bailey. Stop. I don't want you to regret anything that you say tomorrow." With an efficiency that showed he'd done this before, he unzipped my pencil skirt and then turned his back while simultaneously handing me a pair of leggings. "Put these on."

I took them from him, but then I swayed. My stomach roiled, and suddenly I didn't feel so good. "Hunter? I feel a little sick."

He whirled back around and studied me, his eyes intense. "Okay, off to the bathroom."

He carried me. Had I been sober, I would've known enough to be embarrassed. Right now, I didn't really care. When he set my feet down on the cool tile in my bathroom, I swayed again.

Hunter's hands eased into my hair, and he gently pulled the strands back off my shoulders.

Even as he tucked my hair behind my ears, my stomach screamed at me as if to say, *Bitch, next time don't have three shots of vodka. Because why?*

I meant to kneel down to the toilet, but I misjudged the distance. So when my stomach finally give up the fight, cramping and trying to eject everything I'd imbibed, I partially got the sink, but mostly I got Hunter.

Could this get any worse?

———

Hunter

Fuck me.

No, seriously, I really wished she would fuck me.

I looked up at the ceiling and inhaled deeply three times. Ever since Bailey Jones had shown up at Bold Horizons, I'd had a perpetual state of blue balls. And I was certainly going to need balls of steel to deal with this situation.

How is this even happening?

First of all, Bailey thought I was hot? From the get-go, she'd made it a point to ignore any flirting from anyone in the office. When I hadn't immediately come on to her, she'd seemed relieved, and actually become my friend.

I hadn't meant for things to work out quite that well. Yes, of course I wanted to get to know her, but I'd been trying to give her space before asking her out.

It was a new tactic for me. Normally, I had zero problems with women. I looked at them, they knew I wanted them, they smiled back, and usually approached him. Or at least, when I approached, there was no hesitation, no question. Everybody was there for the party.

But with Bailey, things were different. For starters, I worked with her, and I knew better than to shit where I ate. Even if some of the girls there were beautiful, it wasn't worth the hassle.

Secondly, I *liked* her. She was smart, funny, and had this way of putting me completely at ease. She didn't take herself too seriously. It didn't matter how shitty my day was; the moment she smiled, or laughed, or started telling me some ridiculous story, I immediately relaxed. If anything went wrong in my life, Bailey was my first call. Somehow, the girl I'd been trying to sleep with had become my best friend. I had it bad.

Someone was coming for my player card any moment now.

Deal with the problem at hand. Right now, Bailey was trashed. Completely and totally obliterated. Oh, and she'd thrown up all over me, so there was that. A shower was needed for both of us. How the hell was I going to manage this?

I gritted my teeth. "Bay, we need to get in the shower."

She sloppily grinned up at me. "Now you're talking."

Oh hell. The things she was saying. If I didn't know better, I'd think she wanted me. But no, she was drunk. Bailey with all her sober senses would never say any of these things. Didn't matter though, my dick was harder than iron.

Apparently, even though I knew she didn't mean it, my dick hadn't gotten with the program. I was here to be best-friend Hunter. Not I-want-to-fuck-you-in-the-shower-up-against-the-wall-until-you-scream-my-name Hunter. *That* Hunter was on hiatus. At least for Bailey, he was.

Oh, I dated, but casually. *Very* casually. Because I usually found the women I went out with lacking within one or two dates. After all, they weren't Bay. Dammit, I had a real problem.

My dick twitched as if to say, *Damn straight, you do.*

I sighed. "Bay, you're going to finish getting undressed. Can you cooperate with me while we get this done?"

She nodded at me and gave me a happy smile. God, that smile. Sometimes it was the most perfect thing about my day.

I shed my clothes, but left on my boxer briefs. Next came the rest of Bailey's clothing. I did the best I could without looking.

Her stockings nearly did me in. She was wearing thigh highs with delicate lace at the top. I knew the memory of peeling those down her long legs would be forever imprinted in my spank bank.

Once she tossed away her blouse, she stood there in the flimsiest pair of silk panties and some gravity-defying bra that only covered about half her breasts. She looked like she was going to spill out of it at any second, and it sure as shit didn't help that the damn thing was lacy and see-through.

With a dry mouth I muttered, "Get in."

She giggled. "I thought you were joining me."

Fuck. I *was* joining her, but I needed a second to get my erection under control. I climbed in after her, and the water hit us both. She peeled off her bra and revealed the most perfect pair of tits I'd ever seen in my life. Milky skin. Rose-tipped nipples. *Jesus H. Christ.* My imagination offered all the things I could do with breasts like hers. Hold them, weigh them, play with them, lick them...fuck them.

Shit, that was really not helping.

I just needed to get this done and touch her as little as possible.

I grabbed her sponge and handed it to her before squirting shower gel on it. "Start washing yourself."

Bailey made a face. "I want *you* to wash me."

Me too. But that wasn't going to happen.

"Bay, follow directions. I'll start with your hair." I found her shampoo, some raspberry-scented organic something or other. As a stream of water hit my back, I let it hit the back of her hair so the water would drench it. And that was when I noticed. She'd removed her underwear, too.

"Bay, what happened to your panties?"

She glanced at me over her shoulder and winked. "Well, I was wet."

I swallowed hard. "We're in the shower. We're both wet."

She shook her head. "That's not what I meant."

I. Was. So. Fucked.

I shampooed her hair as quickly as I dared, lathering and making sure it was nice and clean. I stepped aside, letting the spray drench her hair, and helping her rinse it out. All the while she kept lazily rubbing soap over her body. Jesus Christ, I wanted to help so badly, but that was a slippery slope.

Standing here, trying desperately to look at the ceiling while I knew she soaped her tits, tested the limits of even my control.

Once her hair was rinsed out, I added the leave-in conditioner and gently worked it through her hair. She moaned, low and throaty, and my dick threatened to come without my fucking say so.

I could do this. I was the good guy. The sexually charged Hunter—the one who was demanding in bed, and got what he needed—I wasn't that Hunter when I was with her. Because I cared about her. I had to remember that.

After I gently took the brush through her hair from the tips to the roots as she instructed, she turned to face me, and I pinned my gaze directly over her shoulder and to the other side of the wall.

"Hunter, I just wanted to say thank you. Sorry I threw up."

I shook my head. "Not your fault. You had a hell of a trauma tonight. And so you overdid it. No big deal. We've all been there."

She pressed her body into mine and—what do you know?—my dick pulsed in my boxers. And then, ever so helpfully, Bailey rubbed her soapy tits on my chest. I let out a low groan that was part growl, and struggled with the reins of my control. But it wasn't until she wrapped her delicate hand around my boxer-clad cock that I lost it.

"Bailey, stop. One day soon, we're going to redo this whole scene. When that happens, I will have you turn that hot little ass around, plant your hands on the wall, and then I will bury my dick inside you. But right now is not that time."

She pouted, but she didn't release me. "But why not? You obviously want me."

"And you are obviously trying to get a spanking."

Her eyes fired wide, but her pupils also dilated. Well, well. It looked like Bailey was totally down for a spanking. Why did that make me want to give her one even more? Lucky for me, she wasn't too keen on listening. She shimmied and pressed her tits into me farther.

"Bailey. Last warning. You need to quit or you will feel my handprint on your ass."

"Hunter. I think I like this dominance in you." She kissed my chin and added a little slip of her tongue as a way to torment me.

I didn't mean to do it, but I couldn't help myself. I firmly set her away from me, turned her around and placed her hands on the opposing wall. Leaning over her back, my dick tented my boxers and pressed into the soft flesh of her ass.

When I whispered, my voice was low, "I warned you. Enough is enough." The crack of my palm over her ass surprised us both. She gasped, but then moaned low. The tingling started at the base of my spine.

No. No. No. I was not going to fucking come right now. Not okay. But I was walking away with one piece of knowledge tonight. Bailey Jones liked dominant Hunter. And I was done being a nice guy.

I took the little sponge and scrubbed myself off in seconds while I kept her in that position. I quickly washed down her back and legs, but at that point, my movements were perfunctory. In seconds, I had us both out of the shower. I wrapped us both in towels and left her briefly to go toss our clothes in the dryer.

When we had both toweled off, I marched her into the bedroom, and handed her a ratty T-shirt from her bottom drawer. I dragged it over her head before pulling back the covers and waiting for her to get in.

"Are you joining me?"

I shook my head even as my cock made an attempt to escape the towel slung around my hips. "No. But don't worry, Bay, we're going to do this again real soon. And next time, I'm going to enjoy making your ass red. I promise I'll make sure to kiss it all better." I ignored her soft gasp and left her in the bedroom while I headed to the living room to watch TV and wait for my clothes to dry.

Once I was dressed again, I let myself out of her apartment. One good thing had come from tonight: now I knew exactly how to handle Bailey Jones.

5

———

Bailey

When I woke up the next morning, it was with the distinct sense that I should be mortified. My head was cloudy and my mouth tasted like old laundry, which was a dead give-away. I'd had way too much to drink last night.

Then I had a flashback of grabbing Hunter's dick in the shower. *Oh, God.*

I sat up slowly, moaning as my stomach rebelled against the motion. What time was it? The memories from the prior day started coming back, and my shoulders sagged when I remembered that it was a Saturday. How could I have forgotten? I'd been pissed to be at the office late on a Friday, and that was how the whole thing had started. I grimaced as I remembered why I'd run out of the office like a hound of death was on my heels.

I'd seen Mr. Dent and his extremely small, ahem, *dent*. Then I'd taken my clusterfuck of a day and doubled down by getting drunk and climbing all over my best friend. He'd been so nice about it, too. Didn't that make it all the worse? I'd basically sexually assaulted the poor man, and he'd just put me to bed like a naughty child.

Grateful that the horrible mini-Dent incident had at least taken place on a Friday, I got out of bed and struggled through a shower. There was a load of things I needed to do around the house. I could keep myself busy by catching up on my to-do list and not even think about the massive cringe-fest that was waiting for me Monday morning. I couldn't afford to lose this internship. I needed the college credit and the recommendation if I'd have any chance of getting a job after graduation and making it into a good MBA program.

I'd have to face Mr. Dent like nothing had happened and smile the whole time. *Ugh.* Then I'd have to face Hunter like I hadn't thrown myself at him and then been rejected. *Double ugh.*

I was in the middle of doing my second load of laundry when the first text from Hunter came in.

Hunter: Hey, how are you feeling today?

I ignored it. I wasn't quite ready to exchange cute text messages about my ridiculous behavior last night. Maybe one day in the future we could joke about it. The distant, distant future. Perhaps by then I'd have forgotten that my friend Hunter had shredded abs, and was totally an alpha male in the bedroom. It was something I wouldn't have thought I'd like, but that had totally turned me on last night. I rubbed my ass. It was still slightly sore from when he'd spanked me. My face flooded with heat and my panties got damp instantly.

Then he texted again.

Hunter: Hope you took the aspirin I left next to the bed.

I frowned. He'd left medicine for me? I hung my head. He really was a sweetheart. No wonder I'd come on to him so hard. It wasn't something I'd usually admit, but Hunter really was my ideal man. Handsome, intelligent, and humble. A killer triple-threat combo that would make any woman instantly dream of wedding bells. But that didn't mean I wanted him to know that I secretly lusted for him.

"This sucks!"

I stabbed at the button on the washing machine to turn it on. Everything was going to be ruined now. The whole reason my friendship with Hunter worked so well was because there was none of the weird flirting that usually ended up wrecking male-female friendships. He'd always been perfectly respectful and I had made sure to treat him the same way. Until last night. How did you go back from a drunken dick grab? He'd seen me naked. I'd asked him to *wash* me. It didn't get any more blatant than that. Now when he saw me, he was always going to think about the things I'd done and said when I was drunk.

My phone rang and the sound startled me. Hunter's picture flashed on the screen, and the image of that perfect face taunted me.

Aren't you glad you ruined our friendship?

Now things are going to be awkward.

Thanks for grabbing my dick, but I don't like you that way.

Not that Hunter would ever say those things, but wasn't that really what it all came down to? I had done stupid things while drunk before, and that was why I usually kept a close eye on how many I had at happy hour. Vodka was a fickle friend, and I didn't enjoy waking up and not knowing where I'd been the night before. Even though I usually brushed things off pretty easily, I couldn't just brush this off.

The reason it was so embarrassing was because I liked Hunter and he didn't like me back.

I managed to dodge his calls the rest of the day and

all of Sunday. He'd even sent a text message threatening to come over, so I'd thrown on sweats and a baseball cap and gone grocery shopping. But now it was Monday morning and as I rode the elevator up to my floor, there was nowhere for me to hide.

At least I probably wouldn't see Hunter until lunchtime. He was one of the best client associates at the firm—everyone said so—and as a result, was always extremely busy. At least I'd have a few hours to figure out what to say to him.

I walked up to my cubicle and gasped. Hunter was sitting in my chair.

"Good morning, Bailey." His eyes took in my slim skirt and the artfully applied makeup that I normally didn't bother wearing.

"Morning," I muttered, taken completely off guard.

What the hell? I hadn't expected him to ambush me, although I probably should have. One of the reasons everyone said Hunter was on the fast track was because he was relentless when working on something. He didn't let anything stop him from getting what he wanted.

"I just wanted to make sure you were okay after getting abducted by aliens. Or being struck down with the plague." At my confused look, he crossed his arms. "What other reason could you have for avoiding me for two days?"

I wasn't going to touch that question. If Hunter wanted to pretend he didn't know why I was embarrassed, I was more than happy to play along. I wanted nothing more than to forget the past week. Amnesia sounded pretty good to me. I dropped my bag next to my desk.

"I had a lot of stuff to do this weekend. A lot of...cleaning."

Hunter snorted. "So that's how we're playing this? You're going to pretend that you didn't show me those perfect tits and give me a permanent case of blue balls?"

———

Hunter

I watched as Bailey's face went red. Damn, she was a sexy little thing, especially when she was flustered.

She glanced around nervously to see if anyone had overheard. Luckily, there was no one nearby. I'd gotten here early, figuring she'd try to sneak in before everyone else, and then go hide in the bathroom.

"Perfect tits? Blue balls?" Bailey whispered. "What are you talking about?"

I shook my head and stood. Her eyes followed as I buttoned my suit jacket. Bailey pressed her thighs together and I smiled knowingly. She may not have wanted to admit it, but she was just as affected by me as I was by her. And I knew I looked good naked. I dedicated a lot of time in the gym to making sure of that.

"You know exactly what you did to me. You're a little tease, Bailey."

"What?" Bailey just blinked at me. Then she seemed to find her usual sass and pointed a finger at me. "You rejected me. You left me alone in my bed when I think I made it really clear that I was open for pretty much anything." She blushed again.

So that's what was going on. She was pissed that I hadn't taken what she'd offered. I grinned. If she only knew. We were just getting started.

"Bailey, we are friends. And yes I have nightly fantasies of you on your back, my head between your thighs, but that doesn't mean that's all I care about."

Her mouth fell open. "You... You think about..."

"Yes. I think about that. A lot. But Friday night, you were upset. You were intoxicated. What you needed was a friend. And I will always take care of you because I want what's best for you."

I leaned closer until I could smell the scent of her shampoo. It didn't escape my notice that her breathing had gotten noticeably faster. She was so responsive.

"Thank you, Hunter." Bailey smiled sheepishly. "I

should have known that was why. You're a really good guy."

"Not that good. Because going forward, what's best for you will be when I put you over my knee and spank that sexy ass."

Bailey's mouth fell open.

I knew I needed to set the tone before she could say anything else. If Bailey had her way, we'd be dancing around the damn friend zone for years before we got anywhere. I wasn't going to let that happen. She was too damned sexy, and not sucking on those perfect tits was practically a crime against nature.

Not to mention the fact that I just wasn't that fucking nice of a guy.

"This is how this is going to work. You're going to sit at your desk like a good girl and do your work. But once this day is over, that ass is mine."

Bailey let out a little moan that instantly made my dick hard. She was enjoying this. The flush of red in her cheeks and the sparkle in her eye proved it. I filed that away for future reference. It was good to know she could appreciate my filthy mouth, because I had no plans of reining it in while fucking her.

"What does that mean?" Bailey finally asked. She smoothed a hand down her skirt, and I noticed that her hand stopped dangerously close to her pussy.

I chuckled. I bet that little kitty cat was soaking wet right about then.

"It means that you are going to leave at exactly five o'clock and head over to my place. And then we're going to have a long overdue conversation."

She gulped. "What if someone sees us leaving together? Won't we get in trouble? I thought employees weren't supposed to date."

"I don't give a damn if someone does see us. What are they going to do, fire me? They'd lose their minds without me here cleaning up their messes inside of a day."

It wasn't arrogance that reassured me that my job was ironclad. My immediate manager was lazy as hell, and none of the other associates had the rapport with the clients that I did. So anyone who had a problem with what I did in my private time could kiss my ass.

"If you're worried about getting in trouble, don't be. We're friends, right? Friends can give their friends a ride home. Besides, I have an offsite at 3, so I'll meet you there."

Bailey nodded. "And after we talk, then you'll take me home."

Hell no, I wasn't taking her home. I knew exactly what would happen if I did that. She'd be inside and ignoring my calls again, and nothing would be resolved.

I needed to get Bailey somewhere we could hash things out, and then we could get down to the good stuff. Such as exactly what she had on under that skirt.

"No, that's not what's going to happen, baby girl."

I reached out and caressed her cheek, unable to stop myself from touching her. Bailey closed her eyes at my touch and made a sound that reminded me of a kitten purring, which definitely didn't help the blue balls situation.

If I was going to get through an entire day of work while thinking about Bailey naked then I needed something to tide myself over. Before she could see it coming, I leaned forward and brushed my lips over hers. When I pulled back, she was gazing at me with needy eyes.

I blew out a breath. I took a step back to keep myself from grabbing her. It was easier to breathe without her warm, vanilla scent wrapped around me.

"You're coming over, we're going to talk properly, and then we're going to see if you need that spanking or not."

I walked away while I still could. This was going to be one long fucking day.

6

———

Bailey

No way was I going along with this.

This was Hunter.

My best friend, Hunter.

Hot Hunter.

No. I wasn't going. I couldn't. Besides, when had Hunter turned into this totally hot alpha guy? No way, no how was I into any of that dominance and being tied up stuff, but, what he'd just said...it was a total turn on.

I inadvertently squeezed my thighs together, trying to quell the throbbing between my legs. Right about now, I was desperate enough to let him do whatever he wanted to me.

All weekend, I'd been thinking about what had

happened. I hadn't been drunk enough to completely forget. How could I? I'd lost my mind and thrown myself at him.

And true to form, Hunter had been a gentleman. Sort of.

Every time I remembered how he'd spanked me in the shower, my clit lit up like a pinball machine. Kind of like now.

I plastered my hands on my cheeks and tried not to think about it. This was insane. How was this Hunter? What happened to nice guy, affable, Hunter? He was sweet, considerate, someone I could really talk to. And he gave me excellent advice. We were friends. *Oh yeah? Do you come on to all your friends like that?*

Okay, there might have been that teeny tiny lapse in judgment. I'd been super vulnerable, more than a little drunk, and suddenly realized my bestie was hot. That wasn't my fault. And with my mind reeling from what I'd seen, and unfortunately heard, I'd been looking for comfort in all the wrong places. So I couldn't really be blamed for suddenly noticing Hunter was hot and then throwing myself at him.

Okay, I could be.

What was I going to do? If I went to dinner at his place, I'd likely need a large glass of wine to fortify myself. And then what would happen? Would we hang out as usual? Would he pick me up, slam me against the wall and drag orgasm after orgasm out of me? God, I hoped so.

No. No, I did not hope so. What was wrong with me?

I wasn't looking for a relationship. Okay, it would be nice to have someone to care about me. But I wasn't looking for something at work. And certainly *not* with my best friend. Because if things went sideways, then who would I talk to? And since when did Hunter want me?

I flushed. Okay, if I was being honest, I'd seen his interest back in the early days. But because I'd been so shut down to any of that, he'd stopped sending the signals, and we'd settled into our friendship.

If I did this, we would be crossing a line we couldn't come back from But what if he was still Hunter? What if we stayed friends, but just added amazing sex? I had no doubt sex with Hunter would be amazing.

There was no way I could do a friends-with-benefits arrangement with him. Friends-with-benefits quickly turned from good, great, awesome benefits to bad bene-fits. Things went wrong. I wasn't going to risk that. He was too important to me.

Okay, yeah, my decision was made. As much as I might want him, as much use as I'd been giving my battery-operated boyfriend, I wasn't going to go there.

So what if he suggested he might spank me or that I might like it? So what if his hands gripping my hips tight had been the hottest thing I'd felt in years? None of that mattered, because I was not going to fuck Hunter.

Besides, given that streak of dominance, I wasn't down for any of that. No man told me what to do. Never mind that I sort of liked it.

Just as I was grabbing my bag to head to the gym before going home, my work phone rang. Mr. Dent. *Crap.* I knew how this was going to go. Instead of getting a workout and going home with takeout to watch reruns of *Sex and the City*, I was going to be here. Working. With Mister Pervy.

"Yes, Mr. Dent?"

"Bailey, I'm reviewing the marketing campaign we just turned in, and none of this is going to work. I need you to stay late. Make a couple of orders from the place around the corner for takeout, but do not exceed fifty dollars."

What the hell? I wasn't even assigned to the Higgins client. And fifty dollars was not going to cover takeout for more than three people if all the interns were working. But he knew that. He was just a cheap ass.

"Okay, sir. How many of us will be staying?" I waited with bated breath, dreading the answer.

"All the interns. This is an all-hands-on-deck situation."

I exhaled a long sigh, then said, "Sure thing." After I hung up with him, I dragged out my cell phone and started a text to Hunter.

Me: Sorry not going to make it. Have to work. Dentface is on a rampage. Rain check?

I had absolutely zero intention of getting a rain check, but he didn't need to know that.

———

Hunter

I stared at the text for several seconds.

She may have had to work, but I knew her well. She'd had no intention of ever coming tonight.

I smirked at my own joke. Well, if she wasn't coming, she wasn't going to give me the brush off via text. She was going to tell me to my face. I wasn't letting her run.

Not after what happened Friday. I knew she wanted me. And I wanted her too. So bad my balls were a permanent shade of indigo. But I wanted more than sex. I wanted *all* of Bailey. This wasn't going to be a casual-sex situation. We could make this thing work. I just had to make sure she saw it too.

Sitting back and being Mr. Nice Hunter had gotten me nowhere. I'd spent a lot of time tamping down my desires and what I really wanted to make someone else more comfortable. Well, I was done with that. I wanted Bailey, so I was going to go get her.

I grabbed a box of her favorite chocolate truffles, which I'd been saving for tonight. If I knew Dent, he might not feed the team he had working. Or if he did, he'd make a point to order less food than was enough for the people there.

At least these would tide her over until I brought her home and could feed her properly.

In minutes, I was out of my apartment and hailing a cab. I lived downtown, so it made no sense to pull out my car when the office was just on the other side of downtown. I could've walked, but I wanted to be quick just in case she did leave the office and try to head home instead.

When I reached the office, I was surprised to find it still hopping and busy with interns working on finishing touches for the Reverence Airlines campaign.

The strange thing was that the interns that were here were lower-level interns, the kind that could make copies and fetch coffee. Bailey might still be an intern, but after working here for nearly a year, she was acting as a junior associate on a lot of campaigns. This campaign wasn't even one of hers. Why the hell had Dent had her stay for this?

Besides, while Dent was technically the person she reported to, the structure was cross-functional. All the projects she worked on were in my department, so why was she staying to help with this stuff?

Because Dent has the hots for her. That made me shudder. I still had the video from the other night. I didn't think Bailey even knew she'd recorded the whole thing. The real question was what the hell was I going to do with it? Right now, I was holding on to it just in case we needed it later.

Okay, first things first. I texted my boss, Stephen, with a quick request to have Bailey help me out with something. Then I marched into Dent's office. This should be fun.

"Hey, Mr. Dent."

Dent frowned. "Hunter? I didn't know you were working late."

"Yeah. Had a little trouble with the Wendell campaign. Actually, can I grab Bailey? She's done most of the original work on it, since she's been working with our team."

Dent frowned. "But I need her here."

And here was the crux of it. I didn't want to have to do this, but I would to get what I wanted.

"Well, you have lots of interns. Bailey's actually done work for my client. So do you really need her to collate, or can another intern handle that?"

Dent's face went red. I had him by the balls. He didn't need Bailey tonight. Bailey didn't even work on this particular project. So having her here was bullshit and we both knew it.

After a few moments, Dent said, "Fine. But I want to talk to Stephen about her time. She is my direct hire."

I smiled. "Oh, I totally get it. The thing is, we have cross-functional teams for a reason, right?"

Let him chew on that for a minute. Bailey wasn't here to be his personal assistant.

"Fine. Use her."

As if the asshole had any right to her. "Thanks." I was sure to keep my voice chipper. After all, I was taking the woman of my dreams to dinner. Like she deserved.

When I found her, she was hunched over her desk, reviewing two different stacks. "Come on, I've sprung you."

She blinked up at me as if unsure she was really seeing me. "Hunter?"

"Yep, in the flesh. Now get your stuff before Dent changes his mind."

She frowned. "What did you do?"

"Nothing. I merely reminded him that you don't

actually do any work for this campaign. So him having you stay is ridiculous. And I got Stephen to give me an out. I said I needed you on my project."

"Hunter. You can't do that."

I nodded. "But I can. If I need an intern, I can ask for one. And I asked for you. So I can, and I did. Now get your stuff, unless you want to stay here all night collating for a client you don't work with, checking for duplicate pages." I put up my hands. "Hey, I thought I was rescuing you, but maybe you're happier here."

After that, she didn't hesitate. She grabbed her bag and then signaled one of the other interns to come and take the stacks from her. And then she was scurrying out behind me.

"Thank you. I thought I was going to go blind in there."

"What are friends for? Now, let's have dinner."

The elevator door dinged open and I stepped in. Bailey hesitated as she followed. "Listen, Hunter, I appreciate the rescue. You have no idea how much. But I don't think dinner at your place is a really good idea."

"Look, I know Dent. He doesn't order enough food and you're probably starving." I pulled out the truffles and gave them to her. "These will tide you over until we get to my place."

She licked her lips as she stared at the truffles. "Who says we're going to your place?"

"I do. We have a date, remember?"

She flushed. "Hunter. You didn't ask me for a date. You *told* me we were having one. I don't like being told what to do."

I leaned over, crowding her a little. She took an automatic step back, but she didn't have very far to go before she hit the wall of the elevator. I kept my voice low and asked, "Are you sure you don't like it?"

Her breath came out in choppy pants. "Hunter, I just—" Her gaze suddenly focused on my mouth and her tongue peeked out to lick her lips.

I barely bit back a groan. Did she have any idea how sexy she was? "Yes, Bailey?"

"Hunter, this—"

I leaned in closer, dipping my head down as if I was going to kiss her. Shit, who was I fooling? I almost did. I forgot that this was all about the tease, and making her want me.

My lips hovered just over hers. "Just tell me you don't want this."

I pulled back a little; she was panting hard now. As I watched the erratic rise and fall of her breasts, my hands itched to palm them.

"I—" she swallowed hard. Then tried again. "Hunter, I can't think when I'm around you."

"Good. Now you know how I've been feeling since you showed up here." When the elevator dinged open, I took her hand. "Come on. You need to eat and we need to talk."

She hesitated for a moment, but then nodded. "Yeah. I guess we do need to talk."

Right now, I needed to do a lot more with her than talk, but we would start with that. And bonus, she was holding my hand, clasping it tightly, like I was her lifeline. I loved the feeling. Without hesitation, I hailed a cab.

She was mine. She just didn't know it yet.

7

———

Bailey

As soon as we arrived at Hunter's apartment, I parked myself on the couch. I'd been to his place plenty of times before, but it had never seemed *this* small.

Hunter, however, seemed to have no issues. I watched as he moved around the living room, turning on lights. He'd hung his coat on the hook by the door and rolled his sleeves up. Even the sight of his bare forearms was hot.

What was that about?

I shrugged out of my coat and tossed it over the back of the couch. Usually when I went over his place, we just hung out, ate pizza, and bitched about work. It was so weird to be here now that he'd seen me naked. I cringed. Worse, he'd seen me naked and barfing, and had to physically peel me off him. *Fantastic.*

"Is Chinese okay?" Hunter's voice interrupted my thoughts.

I nodded frantically. "Yeah, uh huh. Sure, whatever you want."

He looked at me strangely before pulling his phone out of his pocket. While he called the order in, I had to give myself a stern lecture about acting normal.

Just be cool. This is no different than the million other times you've hung out. Yes, you embarrassed yourself the other day, but Hunter is a nice guy. He's not going to rub your face in it.

I felt a little better after that thought. Hunter *was* a nice guy. There was a reason I liked him so much and secretly fantasized about him, after all. He was not only whip smart but he had a great sense of humor, and he just... got me. He would never want to hurt my feelings or embarrass me. I let out a long breath.

Hunter put his phone in his pocket and sat on the couch next to me. We were both quiet for a few minutes and then he turned to me.

"So, we need to talk about what happened the other night."

I groaned. *Okay, scratch that. Hunter is an asshole.*

"No, we don't. I'm totally on board with pretending that never happened."

He leaned closer, crowding me until I couldn't ignore his warm sugar and sandalwood scent. "I'm not okay with that. Damn it, Bailey. You can't just get naked and grab my dick and then act like nothing happened."

Hearing his version of events somehow made it all worse. Mortification flowed over me like lava. I covered my eyes with my hands. Maybe if I didn't have to see him, I could pretend this conversation was happening to someone else.

"I told you I was sorry about that."

I wasn't much of a drinker usually and this was a perfect example why. I didn't like being out of control and I sure as hell didn't like making a fool of myself. An image of me rubbing my bare breasts against Hunter in the shower flashed through my mind, and I groaned as a new wave of shame returned.

"I'm never drinking vodka again!"

Hunter chuckled. "I'll believe that when I see it. And I don't want you to be sorry."

I peeked between my fingers. "You don't?"

"Hell, no." He sent me a look that was hot enough to instantly incinerate my panties.

I clenched my thighs together. Hunter had never looked at me like that before. Was he thinking about what I looked like naked right now? Was he as hot as I was, remembering what we'd almost done?

Then I realized that despite us being just friends, Hunter was still a guy. He probably figured if I was looking to get laid, why not? Why else would he suddenly be looking at me like a lollipop he wanted to taste? He just wanted to hit it and quit it, and I'd made it seem like I was open to that.

"Look, Hunter. I think we should just forget what happened. We're friends. Good friends. And I don't want this to ruin everything. I'm not into just screwing whoever comes along."

Hunter frowned and looked hurt. "That's not what I thought at all." He looked like he was about to say something else, but the doorbell rang just then. He cursed, but got up to answer it.

I let out a sigh of relief. Maybe if we focused on eating, we could get past all this weirdness and go back to the way things used to be.

Hunter returned with the food, and for the next twenty minutes, we were completely consumed with doling out portions from the various containers of food. I finally started to relax when Hunter dug into his beef and broccoli, and showed no interest in talking about our almost-sex the other night.

Maybe it would be fine and I'd been worried for nothing.

But after he'd cleaned up all the remnants of our dinner, he sat next to me, and I could tell he wasn't done exploring the topic.

God, I'd created a monster.

"So you're really going to pretend like that night didn't mean anything?" Hunter asked. His tone of voice indicated that he thought I was full of shit, but was trying hard not to say so.

I sat up on the couch slightly. If we were going to hash this out, I needed to be forceful. Otherwise, I had a feeling he'd bring it up every time I saw him.

"Look, Hunter. That was a mistake, and I know it was confusing to you and I apologize for that. You shouldn't have had to deal with me when I was drunk and horny. I don't know why I was acting like that. In fact, I barely remember it."

"Oh really? Hmm." Hunter eyed me curiously. "So you think you would have reacted that way to just anyone?"

"Probably," I lied. "I was clearly out of my mind. It didn't mean anything."

Hunter grinned. "Really? Well, if you think so, then you won't mind putting it to the test."

"What does that mean?" By the hungry look in his eyes, I had a feeling I knew *exactly* what he meant.

———

Hunter

I had always considered myself a pretty good judge of character. Liars were easy to spot if you knew what you were looking for, even skilled ones.

Bailey was *not* a skilled liar.

She swallowed nervously and I watched with interest as her throat moved. Hiding a groan, I reached down and tried to adjust my suddenly hard dick inside my pants. Fuck, I was turning into a sick son of a bitch if I was getting off just at the sight of her throat working. But I couldn't deny that it brought to mind a fantasy of Bailey on her knees, swallowing around my swollen cock.

She wasn't doing anything so pleasurable in real life though. Oh no, right now she was glaring daggers at me that were so sharp I almost ducked.

"What do you mean, *a test*?"

I figured this was the time to tread carefully. Bailey could be unpredictable, and I was trying to get her closer, not scare her away. But she also couldn't resist a challenge; something I had no problem using to my advantage.

"Well, you said you were out of your mind and didn't know what you were doing."

"I didn't," Bailey insisted before crossing her arms.

Danger. Danger. Alarms were blaring in the back of my mind but I pressed on. I'd been subtle this long and where had that gotten me? Maybe it was time to try a different approach.

"And you said that you would have responded that way to anyone."

"I know what I said, Hunter. Do we really need to rehash this?" She stood abruptly and made a move to grab her bag next to the couch.

Oh, shit.

I jumped up and grabbed her wrist. If she left now, we'd always have this awkward thing between us. And frankly, I wasn't sure I'd survive, never knowing if things could be as hot between us as they'd been in that drunken shower kiss.

"Let me go, Hunter."

"I can't. Because I need to know. Kiss me again. We're both sober now. Then we'll see what's real and what's not."

Bailey's mouth fell open and a tinge of pink appeared in her cheeks. Interesting. She wasn't turned off by the idea. That gave me hope. Because there was a little part of me that was afraid she wasn't lying, that she really had been just drunk and horny and willing to hump anything. But a greater part of me suspected that little Miss Innocent had a thing for me, just like I'd had a thing for her ever since they met.

"That's- that's ridiculous!" she stammered. "You're just trying to cop another feel!"

I moved a little closer and her lips parted slightly, her eyes going soft as she regarded him from under lowered lashes. Oh yeah, she was into this. She could protest all she wanted, but the look on her face gave her away. It also bolstered my resolve to have another taste —a sober taste—of Bailey.

I wanted to see that look on her face while she was spread out underneath me.

"I don't think this is such a good idea." Bailey bit her lip and slanted another look in my direction. But then she licked her lips, unconsciously giving away her thoughts. She wanted this. And I found that my new mission in life was to give her what she wanted. Especially when she was eyeing me like a treat she wanted to lick up.

I raised my hand slowly, so as not to startle her. She watched it warily, but let out a soft little moan when I palmed her cheek. Her eyes closed and she turned into my touch.

"I think this is a very good idea," I muttered. "Let me taste you again, sweetheart. I've been dying for another taste ever since that torture session in your shower."

Her eyes popped open, so I made my move before she could say anything. The instant our lips met, I knew I was in trouble.

Fucking hell, she tasted like peaches and sex.

Bailey moaned against my lips and the sound drove me out of my mind. Then I turned my head to get a better connection between us, and that's when everything blazed out of control. Bailey practically jumped into my arms, and then we were kissing like we wanted to inhale each other, while she scratched the hell out of my back. Our mouths fused together, and I wasn't aware of anything other than the slick glide of her tongue against mine, and the fireworks exploding inside my mind.

This was what I'd been missing, the thing I'd always suspected would be between us, and while my mind soared, my dick got harder than ever.

If she walked away from me after this, I wouldn't survive it.

I walked her backward until she bumped up against the wall. All I could do was be thankful it was there, because otherwise, we would have landed on the floor. Neither of us were aware of our surroundings; only of each other, and the way it felt to be in each other's arms.

In that moment, I realized what a mistake I'd made. Not in kissing Bailey (that was nothing short of a miracle), but in thinking that I could walk away unaffected if she turned me down after this.

Because if Bailey didn't want me, it would have been better to never know just how damn good it could be between us.

8

Bailey

Oh, God, yes. I couldn't hold back a moan.

Hunter's tongue slid over mine, demanding that I respond. His big body crowded me. And then he took my hands in one of his and pinned them above me as he licked into my mouth.

This. This was what I needed. And I wanted more of it. And, bonus! Hunter was more than capable of giving me...more. His huge erection pressed against my belly, and I groaned.

Why did it feel so good to have him pressing into me? Why the hell did it feel so good to have him be so take-charge and in control? Why did I crave it?

I didn't *want* to be this woman. I didn't want to need

him to restrain my hands above my head and to make me moan as he sucked at my neck.

Who are you kidding? Yes, you do want this. You do need this. This was Hunter, and like it or not, I'd been fantasizing about him long before the events of last Friday.

That was the truth. I *had* been fantasizing about him. And so what if my vibrator had gotten a lot of use since I'd started working at Bold Horizons? I wasn't admitting that. Not to him, anyway. Because we were just friends.

Oh yeah, you kiss all your friends like that?

My mind tried weakly to restart, to take over the thickening of the lust in my blood. It tried to come online and use rationality to quell the burning need Hunter had sent thrumming inside my body. My brain tried to flush out the lust that was making my skin hum and my body purr. Unfortunately, my brain was losing that battle.

Hunter tore his lips from mine. "You taste so fucking good. I could do this all damn day."

He slid his hand up my torso. Despite myself, I arched into the caress, seeking more, wanting his hands on me. With his other hand, he palmed my breast, gently swiping his thumb over my nipple, and my clit throbbed.

I was going to come. Just like this. With Hunter pressing up against my belly, swiping his thumb over me, I was going to come apart, standing up, backed up against a wall in his apartment. Was I really ready for that?

Quick answer, no. Because Hunter was my friend. And whatever the hell my body wanted to do, whatever the hell I'd managed to convince his body he wanted to do, that line we were crossing was going to break us. I couldn't have that. I *needed* Hunter. He was one of my few true friends at the company, and I wasn't about to ruin that or my career just because Hunter Richards made my panties wet.

With that, my brain finally started to come online, to run through all the reasons why this was a terrible idea. My brain helpfully listed the reasons:

1.The two of us were friends.

2.The morning after had sucked hard. I wasn't eager to repeat that experience.

3.Hunter had one helluva reputation.

He never talked about it, but the interns in the office pretty much swooned whenever he walked by. One of the interns told me that he'd dated a friend of hers. Word was, his dick was huge. *Huge.* Like, world-record sized. From the feel of it, they weren't kidding.

Was I really willing to have my vajayjay stretched out by my best friend? *Yes, absolutely yes.* What? No. Of course not. Not at all.

I slid my hand down his chest and gently shoved. "Hunter. Stop. We can't."

Hunter shook his head and looked like he was battling to open his eyelids. "What? Why the fuck not?"

"I'm sorry. I just can't. We're going to ruin everything if we do this. If you just wanted to prove a point, yes, I remember. I remember everything. But I can't handle this." That was the truth at least. I slid out from under his arm.

"Bailey, wait. Look, if we just talk —"

But I was done talking. I knew what would happen if we talked any more. I was going to climb him like a tree. I was going to sit on that monster dick and demand that he give me orgasms. And that wasn't going to work out well for me. Better to run.

Yes, tomorrow at work would be awkward, but we would manage. As long as we didn't cross this line.

"I'm sorry, Hunter."

I grabbed my purse and made a beeline for the door. I tried not to think about how hurt he looked. I tried not to think about how much my body already missed the press of his skin against mine. No, better not to think about that.

Traffic was a bitch which only worsened my mood. When I finally got home, I let myself into the apartment and went straight for the shower. I could still smell

Hunter's cologne all over me, and I'd have an impossible time sleeping if I didn't wash it off.

After a hot shower that did nothing at all for my knotted muscles, I headed for bed. But the moment I plugged my phone in, it rang. Hunter's smiling face appeared before me, and I scowled. Why couldn't he just let this go?

The thing was, I *wanted* to talk to him. I wanted to regain some of who we were. *Friends*. Friends who were desperately trying to ruin everything we had.

I answered. "Hunter, if this is to somehow get me back to your place, it's not going to work. I said everything I needed to say."

He sighed. "No, Bailey. Let me apologize. I didn't mean for things to get so out of hand. But the moment I kissed you—" he took a deep breath, started again. "Look, all I'm asking for is a shot. Obviously, there's something going on with us. Something more than just being best friends. Just come with me on a date tomorrow night. Somewhere that isn't either of our apartments, and if you don't feel what I feel, I'll leave you alone. We'll never talk about this again. We'll go back one hundred percent to being Bailey and Hunter."

"Hunter, it's not going to be that easy."

"Yes, it will be, because your friendship is more important to me than anything else. But if I have the chance at more with you, then I want to take it. Because just feeling what I've felt the last couple of times we've been together, I have to take the shot."

"Hunter, how are you so sure?"

"I just am. What do you say? Will you let me take you out?"

All I wanted to do was blurt out *yes*, but I was cautious, trying to think it through. If it didn't work out, he'd promised me we could go back to being normal, and I wanted that. So if one date was all it took for us to get on an even keel again, then I was in.

"Okay. Let's go on a date."

Hunter

When was the last time I had been this nervous for a date?

I'd been of two minds about what we should do. Part of me thought I should pull out all the stops: super fancy restaurant, followed by some insane view of the city, followed by some underground speakeasy type of bar. Somewhere cool and intimate where I could turn on the charm.

I wanted all of that for Bailey. I wanted to show her

the moon and stars. But I also wanted to show her that even if things went wrong, we would still have our friendship.

So I was going to skip all that.

I just hoped she liked it. I didn't want to come across as if I wasn't trying. Hell, I was actually trying really hard.

Why is this so important to you?

Because it was Bailey, who I'd been falling for slowly over the last year. Also because a part of me knew she was right. What we had was good. I knew we could be better than good, but I didn't want to fuck this up. So I was gonna go low key. Make her comfortable. And if somehow she didn't want to see me like that, I would deal. I would have to buy some major stock in a porn company, but I'd be okay.

Yeah, you keep telling yourself that.

I picked her up at seven on the nose. When she opened the door, I had to resist the urge to reach out and touch her in all kinds of inappropriate ways.

That afternoon at work, I'd told her to dress casual. For Bailey, that evidently meant tight leather leggings that hugged her ass and her legs, black low-heeled boots, and a pink off-the-shoulder top that clung to her tits in ways that made me want to bury my face between them.

No. The early part of this date was about me and Bailey finding our footing and being able to still be ourselves. Later tonight, I might do just about anything to bury my face in her tits, but right now I wanted to have fun. I wanted us to play.

"So why the mystery? Where are we going?" she asked.

"You know, you're just going to have to trust me."

She wrinkled her nose, but when I offered her my hand, she slid her palm into mine. I tried not to focus too much on how it felt to touch her. I tried not to think about the satin smooth feel of her skin, the charge of electricity running up my arm. No. Right now, all I wanted to think about was enjoying her company...and not where else that satin soft skin would feel good.

It took us a few minutes to get used to each other, and the tension was thick, but I was determined.

When I drove up to the old-fashioned diner, she giggled. "This is not what I expected for dinner."

"Well, I figure any guy can take you to some fancy douchey place." I laughed. "Relax, we're here to play."

"To play, what?"

"Pick a game, any game. Even though this is a date, I will warn you that I will show you no quarter. I'm here to kick your ass."

Immediately, Bailey's competitive nature came out.

"What? You think you're gonna kick my ass in arcade games? You're on."

I laughed. She was so cute every time she got that determined look on her face, with her nose scrunched and her lips pursed slightly. It made me want to kiss her, but that could wait. For the time being, I was here to kick her ass.

Except that was not how it happened. After three rounds of Ms. Pac-Man, King Kong, Ski Ball, and Hoops Shoot Out, we were evenly tied. Why was she so good at these? And how the hell had I not known that?

Usually, we played bar games: trivia, darts, pool. I actually had to try at some of these games. She was a demon at Miss Pac-Man. She'd won all three of those games. King Kong, I won. Ski Ball had been a heated battle and she'd won by one. And Hoops Shoot Out, I'd won by one. Now it was down to Dance Dance Revolution.

I could only pray I wasn't going to get my ass kicked on this. But given the way she unzipped her boots, laid them to the side, and gave me a cheeky grin, I had a feeling an ass whooping was imminent.

I was right. Bailey was not above knocking me over or shoving my feet off of the footpads, and I was pretty sure she made her boobs jiggle a little extra just to distract me. When we were done and she'd beaten me by over a thousand points, I demanded a rematch.

But once again, I got distracted by her jiggling breasts.

"That was hardly fair. I'm pretty sure you were trying to distract me."

"If you can't take the heat, get out of the kitchen."

I shook my head. "Next time we do this, I'll be ready for you."

"If you say so," she giggled.

"Come on, let's go eat."

"Okay."

As I led her past the hostess stand, she jogged to catch up to me. "We're not eating here?"

"I told you. We came here for the games. Now, I'm going to feed you. And find out all the secrets to how you got so good."

"A master never reveals her tricks."

"Yeah, whatever."

Again, I knew I'd surprised her with my dinner pick. We drove up to the food truck, Mini Chef.

"I love this food truck!" she squealed.

"I know. Why do you think I brought you here?"

If she had her pick, she'd spend her entire lunch hour most days driving around looking for it. They had this Korean BBQ sandwich she usually inhaled. I had no idea where she put any of that.

Her smile was warm when she turned to me. "You know, I didn't think you were paying such close attention to me."

"Bailey, when it comes to you, I'm always paying attention. Come on, let's eat."

After our dinner, eaten on the curb next to the food truck, she said, "Thank you. This was actually kind of perfect."

"Well, I do aim to please. But you don't think we're done yet. Do you?"

"Oh, yeah? What does the great Hunter Richards have up his sleeve this time?"

I stood and tugged her hand so that she stood in front of me. "Dessert, of course."

Her pupils dilated, and I bit back a groan. This was the perfect moment to kiss her. And fuck, did I want to. But there would be time enough for that. Right now, I was still in date mode. Once again, I put my hand out, and Bailey took it without hesitation. With her, this was so easy. With her, this was so right. I just hoped that she would see it that way.

9

―――――

Bailey

I was in so much trouble.

I gnawed at my thumbnail, trying desperately to think of anything but how sexy Hunter looked. He'd surprised me by taking me to the arcade. When he'd convinced me that going on a date was a good idea, I'd assumed he planned to impress me. I'd braced myself for a pretentious restaurant with tiny portions that wouldn't satisfy an ant, and for Hunter to morph into someone else; a mirror image of all the other guys who'd tried to get in my pants.

That was really what I was afraid of, I had to admit. Taking our friendship to a different level meant by defi-nition that we had to leave the level we were currently on. I didn't want to leave this level. I *liked* this level. More than anything, I liked knowing that my best friend, Hunter, would be there for me, no matter what.

Now the bastard had done the absolute worst thing in the world. He'd called my bluff and proven to me that dating him didn't mean our friendship would disappear. It would just have a new, exciting layer of sexual tension sprinkled on top.

Which was a wonderful thing, but also completely nerve-wracking.

As we approached my door, my nerves surged once again and I placed a hand against my stomach. It shouldn't be such a big deal—after all, we'd already kissed. Multiple times. But we'd never kissed after going on the most fun date I'd ever been on. We'd never kissed with the knowledge that the fun date was over and it was time to decide if I wanted to take this new aspect of our relationship any further.

But no pressure or anything, right?

"I had a lot of fun tonight," Hunter said as we reached my door. His dark eyes locked on mine and, just like that, all my nerves were back.

"Me too. This wasn't what I was expecting at all, but it was great. Perfect, actually. You're a really nice guy, Hunter."

Instead of the smile I was expecting, his eyebrows

drew together. He cursed softly and his hand tightened around mine. When he looked at me again, I shivered. He was looking at me the same way he had the other times he'd kissed me. Intense. Wanting. Aggressive.

Basically, the opposite of the Hunter I was used to.

He gripped my chin tightly and I let out a soft moan. It shocked me that I enjoyed this side of him. There was no denying how wet it made me when he took control like this.

"Let's get one thing straight, sweetheart. I'm glad you enjoyed our date. I'll always work overtime to make sure you get everything you want and *everything* you need. But I am not," he leaned down until his lips were brushing mine with every word, "that fucking *nice.*"

As soon as he said the word our lips connected. All thought scattered until my whole world was Hunter's mouth devouring mine and his hand cupping my ass through my leggings.

I lost all sense of time and place, no longer caring about anything but feeling his skin against mine. I wrapped my legs around his waist. He grumbled something that I didn't catch, but in the next moment I didn't care what he'd said, because he aligned himself perfectly between my legs and *oh my God, was that really as big as it felt?*

"Bailey, fuck, you feel good, sweetheart. I knew you

would." He continued growling things against my skin in between kisses, and his deep voice sent shivers up and down my spine.

It made me crazy, *he* made me crazy, and I no longer had control of my body. I was no longer running the control tower, because my pussy had taken the reins, and it wanted to feel that monster in his pants come out to play.

I grabbed his hair, holding on for dear life as I rode him like a show pony, rubbing myself against him shamelessly. Even with all the layers of clothes, it felt amazing, and I wondered why the hell we'd taken so long to do this. And why were we wearing clothes, again?

Then I wasn't thinking anything, as fireworks exploded through my body. Jesus Christ. I'd just come. Right in the fucking hallway.

Hunter growled his approval as his hands left my ass. One crept under my shirt and the other found its way into my panties. Oh, Jesus Horatio Christ. When his hands found my breasts spilling over my bra, he moaned. And when his hands moved to my pants and his fingers found me slick, he bit me.

"So fucking sexy, Bailey. You know exactly what you're doing to me, don't you?" He slid two fingers inside me while he teased my nipple. "You could take my big dick right now, couldn't you? You naughty girl."

It came out like an accusation, but apparently he was speaking a language that my pussy understood, because that traitorous bitch just preened at his words as if to say, *Yes, I do like to tease cocks. But it's because they enjoy it so much.* It clenched hard around his questing fingers, and I moaned. I needed more of him.

There was a loud whistle, and we sprung apart at the sound. I shook my head to clear the fog from my brain. Mrs. Potts, a sweet elderly woman who always seemed to wear cardigans no matter the weather, was standing in her doorway watching us.

"Normally I wouldn't be a cock block," she warbled in her reedy voice, "but my grandkids are here and they'll be leaving soon. It's a little early for them to get the birds-and-the-bees talk."

"Oh my God. I'm so sorry, Mrs. Potts!" I turned and grabbed my keys from my purse, which had dropped to the ground during our frantic fumbling. I opened the door to my apartment and Hunter followed me inside, chuckling the whole way.

"It's not funny! We just scandalized my eighty-year-old neighbor!"

Hunter didn't even bother trying to hide his amusement. "In case you didn't notice, she didn't seem all that scandalized. Hell, I'd wager she stood there and watched for a while before she said anything. Besides, she said cock, so how scandalized can she be?"

That thought was even worse than the previous one, so I covered my ears. "I'm not listening."

Hunter grabbed my hands and pulled me against him. I wasn't expecting the sudden motion, so I fell against his chest in an awkward heap.

"Where were we before the interruption?"

As his head lowered toward mine, I knew that this was make-it-or-break-it time. I could either put a stop to it and always wonder how good we could have been together, or I could put my big girl panties on and take a chance.

I looked down at the large bulge in the front of Hunter's pants.

Come on, it taunted. *You know you want to see what I can do. And you really want to see if I'm as big as I look.*

Oh, hell, I thought. You only live once, and I sure as hell wasn't going to live the rest of my life wondering if I'd let the cock of my dreams go by, just because I was afraid of getting hurt.

Plus, if the look in Hunter's eyes was any indication, he knew how to make it hurt real good.

————

Hunter

I watched as Bailey stepped back and whipped her shirt over her head, leaving her in only a black bra and the tightest black leather pants ever invented to torture the male mind.

Instantly, my cock tried to punch through my jeans. I tried to slow my arousal down. I couldn't blow this. I thought of baseball stats, my last marketing campaign, and tried to remember how much horsepower my favorite muscle car had. It was no use: my mind and my cock refused to be distracted from the monumental hotness of Bailey Jones.

Her blond hair was an absolute mess around her head, strands falling over the cleavage spilling from her bra. Her blue eyes stood out against the blush on her cheeks. She looked adorable and somehow naughty at the same time.

"This might be a bad idea, but I officially don't care anymore. I want you, Hunter."

Her voice lowered at the last part into a husky purr and I almost came right then and there.

"Jesus, Bailey. I want you too, sweetheart. But we're not rushing this. I've been dreaming about what I'd do to you if I had the chance for too long."

"You've been dreaming about me?" She twisted a strand of hair around her finger nervously.

Oh hell no, that wouldn't do. I didn't want her nervous and over-thinking things. Luckily, I knew exactly how to take her mind off anything other than how good I could make her feel. That was something else I'd been dreaming about for months.

I picked her up, and she squeaked as she grabbed at my shoulders. I'd been in her place enough times that I didn't need directions. Her bedroom was a girly paradise. I'd watched her getting ready too many times, often fantasizing about pushing her down on that ruffled comforter and burying my face between her legs. I set her on the edge of the bed carefully. Bailey watched me warily as I tugged and pulled until her leather pants were around her ankles. She giggled and kicked them to the floor, then turned and scrambled across the bed, providing a heart-stopping view of her luscious ass.

The devil made me do it. Honestly, I really couldn't help myself. When my palm landed on her ass, her delicate skin pinked and I cursed softly.

"You are really trying to kill me," I mumbled before shedding my own clothes.

When she turned and saw that I was naked, she blushed. "You don't waste any time, huh?"

I shook my head silently, too turned on to bother

with conversation at this point. Without a word, I reached out and gently pulled her down by the ankles until she was right in front of me. With her legs spread open, she looked like a centerfold, all blonde hair, full breasts and smooth skin.

"Oh, wow, you've always been efficient." Bailey moaned as I leaned over her and kissed her neck.

My fingers made quick work of the front clasp of her bra, and then her breasts were free. Her candy-pink nipples beckoned and I took my time lavishing them with soft, suctioning kisses. One day, I'd spend hours just torturing these beauties, but today I had a different destination in mind.

"Hunter... please."

Her soft pleas only kicked my arousal into high gear as she squirmed beneath the path of my tongue. It traveled over her softly rounded belly and then lower. And lower. And...

"Oh my God. Hunter!"

I growled against the soft lips of her pussy, hard as a rock from her response. Her legs fell open shamelessly as I worked her little clit, the tiny bundle of nerves standing up like it was trying to flag down my attention. Well, never let it be said that I didn't give the people what they wanted. I growled again, letting her hear my pleasure at her taste, and her fingers curled into the sheets next to his head.

Oh hell yes, that was exactly what I wanted to see. Watching her response and hearing her helpless little cries as she writhed beneath me made me crazy. I had to rein in my caveman desire to spread her open and fuck her immediately.

Slow down. This is Bailey. We need to take care of her. Make sure she's satisfied.

As she shrieked and her pussy clenched against my mouth, my arguments for slowing down lost some of their power. Especially when her fingers latched onto my ears in a death grip.

"Hunter, please. *Fuck me*, oh, God, I need it."

My cock stood up straight as if to say *Yes, ma'am*. I swept my arm around the floor wildly, praying I'd find my pants. I pulled back slightly and Bailey whimpered at the loss of contact.

"Hold on baby, I'm coming back."

I got a condom on in record time and then I was back between her thighs. She let out a sigh of relief that sent my ego into the stratosphere. Her lashes rested against her cheeks and she looked like an angel.

"Fuck me, Hunter. What the hell is taking so long?"

I chuckled. She was an angel with a dirty mouth.

Before she could berate me anymore, I lifted one of her legs, curled it around my waist, and notched my cock right against her pussy. She mewled at the contact, moving and wiggling like she was trying to force me inside.

"You ready, baby girl?"

Go slow. Go slow. Go slow. I was trying. I really was. But with Bay, it was next to impossible. I knew I was big. I just prayed the two orgasms she'd already had would ease the way. Her frantic nod paused when I bucked my hips and thrust balls deep in one stroke.

So much for going slow.

"Oh fuck." Bailey's hands left the sheets and clamped on my ass cheeks, holding me against her. She shuddered and looked up at me with the most arresting *fuck me* expression.

"You're so big." She hissed in a deep breath.

I held myself still. She felt like a slippery, silken glove around my dick and I prayed I could go slow. "Breathe, Bay. Nice and easy. Are you okay?"

"Yes, that's what I need."

I growled at her words and snapped my hips again, pulling out almost all the way and then burying myself completely in the soft, wet, willing pussy that was begging for me almost as blatantly as her owner.

God. Damn.

I set up a fierce rhythm, fucking her so deep and

hard that her headboard slammed against the wall. Mrs. Potts and all the rest of her neighbors could probably hear it, but I didn't fucking care.

On the next retreat, I pulled out, glancing down at where our bodies were joined. Her lips were so sweet, pink, perfect. One day, I was going to sink into her bare. One day, I was going to come inside her. My cock twitched at the thought.

But today was not that day. Instead, with my fingers, I spread apart her lips, opening her up for me. I notched my dick directly over her clit and proceeded to slide.

Bailey bucked, nearly unseating me, and I couldn't help the smirk. When she started to shake, I slid my free hand to her ass, cupping it and holding her in place as I conducted my slow torture. I squeezed her ass gently, and her eyes rolled back into her skull.

"You like this, Bailey girl?"

"Hunter, oh, God, please—"

I shifted my grip and my finger grazed her sensitive pucker. My eyes flashed to hers even as her hips bucked, and I grinned.

"Hunter?" Her question was soft.

"Not tonight, Bay, but one day, I'm going to have all of you. Would you like that?" I wasn't sure if it was the way my dick slid over her clit, the way my finger gently penetrated her ass, or my dirty promise, but she came hard, her body clamping around my exploring finger.

Wasting no time, I adjusted my position and sank into her again with one smooth stroke. Holy. Fucking. Shit. She was tight. Too tight. And she was gripping my dick like her pussy meant to strangle the life out of it.

Then Bailey was flying again. Or maybe that was one long orgasm. Her nails dug into my shoulders as she chanted my name over and over again.

"Hunter. Hunter. Hunter."

The edges of my vision grayed out and all I saw were stars as I came.

10

Bailey

My ass was cold. I frowned as I reached to pull up the covers. One problem. Okay, two problems. First, the sheets were mostly twisted around my ankles and the comforter only covered my top half, exposing my ass and the backs of my legs to the cool morning air.

Second, when I reached for the covers, every muscle I had ached. Why was I sore like I'd run a marathon? I wasn't the marathon type. If it was anything more strenuous than yoga, I wasn't really down for it. My pussy ached in that delicious too-stretched way.

And then it all came back to me. *Hunter.*

The two of us in the hallway. Hunter leaning over

and kissing me as he slid his hands into my leggings, finding me wet and ready. The orgasm he'd given me as he rocked against me right outside my front door. Never mind bothering to get inside or anything. Nope. Who needed privacy for orgasms?

Once he kissed me, it had been over. I'd had an orgasm *in my hallway* where anyone could see.

Awesome. Now I'd be *that* girl. The one who got off in the hallway.

I groaned as I rolled over, automatically seeking Hunter's warmth. My whole body flushed as I remembered the crack of his palm on my ass. His finger back... there. I'd never done anything like that and it surprised me that I liked it.

The rumors about Hunter were true. He was freaking enormous. But he'd been gentle with me—and rough with me, all at the same time.

I was pretty sure I would have a few love bites and my nipples and my inner thigh muscles were on fire. I could use the time this morning to take a soak. But that would mean leaving Hunter in bed, and I vaguely recalled his offer of morning sex in the shower. *You are a glutton for punishment.* That I was. Just the idea of his hands on me again made me tingle.

When I rolled over to meet the heat, it wasn't there. I didn't dare crack open an eyelid, but I could feel the warm streaks of sunlight already threatening to break through my lids. I patted around on Hunter's side of the bed. Empty.

I eyes snapped open. "Hunter?" Had he climbed into the shower without me? That was hardly fair. Wrapping my comforter around me, I wiggled out of bed, groaning as my clit throbbed and my legs shook. Jesus. What that man could do to me. Some of the things we'd done—some of the places he'd put his tongue—made me flush. But I'd enjoyed every damn second of it.

"Hunter? Where are you?"

I checked the kitchen and living room, and then headed for the shower. Had he forgotten we were supposed to shower together? When I padded into the bathroom, there was no sign of him, and no sign of his clothes, either. He wasn't here.

Even in the face of the evidence, I refused to believe it. No. There was no way he had left me after what we'd done.

Especially not after planning a date like that. That was the guy I knew. The Hunter I loved wouldn't do things like that.

Whoa, easy there. Love?

No. It wasn't like that. I loved him like a best friend would.

Sure, keep telling yourself that. The guy I knew would never fuck and dash.

Except, where was he?

Had he seriously been playing the long game? I knew the guys in the office talked about how I'd shot down pretty much anyone who dared ask me out.

Had Hunter stepped up to the challenge? Of course he had. And now that he'd spoken to me in all the dirtiest ways possible, he was done.

Oh, God.

I sank to the floor with the comforter wrapped around me and leaned my head against the wall to the bathroom. What had I done?

You let that man put his tongue in your— No. I wasn't going to think about it.

But even as I was busy trying not to think about all the places Hunter's tongue had been, and all the ways he'd fucked me, my body heated. And before I knew it, I was wet. Dammit.

Fuck him. *I* was the goddamn prize. He really thought I was going to be another notch on his bedpost? Did he expect me to run? To avoid him? Well, I wasn't going to do that.

What I was going to do was get in the shower, wash my hair, look totally fucking smoking hot, and then have ice cream for breakfast. Because that's what you did when your best friend turned out to be a total asshole.

Once I was out of the shower and had styled my hair into soft, beachy curls, I took time applying my makeup.

In addition to the usual tinted moisturizer and bronzer, I put on lipstick, and even mascara. When he saw me, he was going to eat his heart out. Even better, I wore red: A flirty skirt, paired with a blazer and a silky white camisole. My staggeringly high Jimmy Choos completed the look. I loved those shoes. I'd won them at a radio station's Pick-a-Pair party.

While I stood in my kitchen, eating cookies and cream straight from the carton for breakfast, I tapped my foot and struck a power pose. I was a strong woman. And I wasn't going to let this setback topple me.

If Hunter Richards thought I was going to let him near any of this again, he had better think again.

Hunter

By the time lunch rolled around, I was ready to rip someone's head off.

First, I was starving. Second, I hadn't heard from Bailey all damn day. When I'd gotten the five a.m. urgent call, I'd had a massive urge to throw middle fingers to the air and ignore it. I was finally with Bailey, and nothing could compare to that.

But it was never a good idea to tell the senior vice president to go fuck himself. It turned out that the senior vice president, Stephen, had a dog. And that dog, Daisy, had inhaled our entire Wendell RFP flash drive as part of her breakfast.

And given that we had to present to Wendell at two pm today, we didn't have time for Daisy to release that piece of goodness. Why in the world did Stephen insist on doing things old school? It was like when it came to his technological development, he'd stopped at flash drives. He refused to store anything on cloud storage for fear that someone was going to hack us.

Seriously, who was that daft? Everything we had done was on that one fucking flash drive. Now, we'd all have to piece together what we thought we had. So here we all were, the entire goddamn team, trying to piece together our pitch before everything had to go to the printer at noon. It made for one hell of a rough day.

It was a far cry from how I'd planned to wake up, with my mouth firmly planted on Bailey's pussy, drawing a sheet-clawing orgasm out of her with my tongue, fingers, and eventually, my cock.

Oh, the plans I'd had.

Turned out Bailey slept completely spread out, limbs thrown everywhere, which would have proven useful for my plans. I could've kissed down her stomach, nudged her thighs open wider, licked her softly to wake her up. *The best way possible.*

Of course, that would have been quickly followed with an amazing shower fuck. Maybe I would have had the opportunity to play with her ass again. After seeing her reaction last night, I was quickly becoming obsessed with fucking her in all ways.

But no. Five a.m., my stupid phone rang, and now it was nearly one. I sent another text to Bailey.

Me: Did I break you last night? Your fingers don't work anymore because of the way I had you clawing at the sheets? Let's get lunch and I can kiss them all better...or other things.

I hit send and waited, but nothing came back, and I was starving. A sliver of unease slid over my skin. I'd been checking my phone like a teenage girl waiting for her prom date. Where was she?

My first stop was Bailey's desk. I wanted to play it cool because I didn't want anyone in the office to know about us. That was more for her than me, though, because I would've gladly shouted it from the rooftops. *Listen up fuckers, she's mine.*

But Bailey was an intern, so I understood she might

not want her business out there for everyone to judge and gossip about.

"Hey, beautiful," I whispered. She didn't look up.

I stood there for a good few seconds before I tapped her on the shoulder. "Hey, what's up?" Her head snapped up and she dragged ear buds out of her ears.

"Oh. It's you."

I frowned. Something was wrong. I could see it in the tension around her lips. "You okay? Did something happen?"

She shook her head. "Is there something you need?"

Oh, yeah, I need something all right.

A smirk tugged at my lips. "Well, now that you're asking..." But when she jerked away from my touch, I could see that she clearly wasn't in the mood for jokes. "Come on, something's wrong. Talk to me."

She turned in her seat to face me, and then stood to full height. "Listen, I know you think you're being cute right now but I'm not in the mood. So just let me know what the hell it is you need."

My brows snapped down. "What's going on?" I glanced around to make sure that no one could overhear us. I was lucky that most folks were out to lunch.

Putting my hands on her shoulders, I gave her a gentle push into her seat as I knelt in front of her. "Did I do something? Because last I remember, you were coming around my dick. And when I saw you this morning, you looked happy. Peaceful even. So what's changed?"

Her mouth fell open. "What's changed?" She gave me an exasperated shake of her head. "You know what? This was a huge mistake. I can't believe I let you talk me into this."

The slice of pain cut deeper than I thought it would. "Mistake? Is that why you haven't returned any of my texts today?"

A feeling of dread looped around my neck and started to squeeze. Had I been too rough when I'd spanked her? She'd seemed to like it, but had I read that wrong? And the hickeys. They were probably really showing on her skin now. And that other stuff: the dirty talk, my finger in her ass. I'd pushed her too hard. And I was big, I knew it. She might be sore today.

You're an idiot.

"Did I hurt you last night?" I swallowed hard, unable to get the words out. "Fuck, I'm sorry. I didn't mean to. I just need you to talk to me. Tell me—"

"No, dumbass. You hurt me this *morning*. I mean, I should've known that you were only interested in me for —" she halted and frowned. "What texts?"

I stared at her. "I couldn't find anything to leave a note on. And I didn't want to wake you because, let's face it; I kept you up half the night. So I sent you a text with where I was going, told you I'd see you for lunch. You didn't reply."

Her scowl started to loosen, but her gaze was still narrowed, as if she wasn't sure if she should believe me. "I didn't get a text."

"Check your phone. I sent it to you this morning at 5:15 when I was still in your bed."

"5:15? Where the hell were you going that early?"

I threw my hands up. "I was coming *here*. Check your phone."

She pulled her purse out of the drawer and then dragged out her phone. She didn't even look at it when she held it up to me. "See, no text alerts."

I worked hard to keep my smile in check. "Bay, is your phone on?"

"What? Don't be ridiculous." When she snapped the phone back around and hit the home button, nothing happened. And then she flushed. "Oh, God. After our date, I... didn't take it out of my purse. Because I didn't touch my purse again until this morning to transfer everything to my bag for work."

"And let me guess, you didn't think to charge it?" I pinned her with a direct look.

"No. I was a little preoccupied this morning. I thought you'd abandoned me."

I took her hands. "Bay, why would I do that? That was single-handedly the most intense—" I slid my glance around again, "night of my life. I would never just walk out on you. I wouldn't hurt you like that."

She flushed a deep red. "I know. I—I'm sorry. God, I just woke up and you were gone, and I assumed that you just walked out."

"You think I could walk away from you after last night? You pretty much own my dick. Where you go, he goes. You two are like a package deal now."

She covered her face with her hands. "I'm sorry, Hunter. I feel like a total idiot."

Relief flooded my veins and I brought her hands back down into her lap as I held them. "Hey, I'm just glad you're not kicking me to the curb. Once we get this Wendell thing over with, I'd like a morning after redo if you don't mind."

A smile tickled her lips. "I feel like that might be arranged."

My gaze followed as she flicked out her pink tongue to moisten them. "Good."

Memories of what we didn't get to finish this morning assailed me. "But before I can give you a better morning after, I think we need to make up. Come on."

She followed but asked, "Where are you taking me?"

"Somewhere I can show you how awesome it is to

make up." I needed her now. Needed to chase away the panic I'd been feeling a minute ago. I needed to sink deep inside Bailey so that I could remind her, and myself, that we belonged together.

And I knew just the place.

11

———

Bailey

I moved my legs double time, trying to keep up with Hunter's pace.

"Slow down," I hissed, hoping like hell that no one would come down the hallway and see him dragging me like a madman.

He took an abrupt left and we stumbled through the doorway into the supply closet. The sharp tang of some kind of cleaning fluid assaulted my nose. Before I could say anything about it, Hunter's lips covered mine. Immediately, all rational thought flew from my brain, and all I could do was feel. I tangled my fingers in his hair and massaged the thick strands as I sucked on his tongue.

When I'd woken that morning to an empty bed, it

had hurt way more than I'd told him. He'd done more than just sex me up last night; he'd completely over-whelmed me. There was no denying it: my heart was wrapped up in this. If he wasn't as invested as I was, there was going to be one major fall in my future.

"God damn, I missed this all day. Tell me you missed me." Hunter growled against my neck, and the rumble of his deep voice against my skin sent a chill down my spine.

"I missed you, too. That's why I was so upset."

Hunter's hands tightened on my hips. "I can't believe you thought I would just leave you like that."

Now that he'd explained everything, I felt terrible. He'd looked so hurt that I hadn't had more faith in him. I really couldn't explain why my mind had immediately gone straight to assuming he was a douche. Was I so used to assholes that I didn't know a good guy when I had one? I hated the idea that my past dating history could be screwing up a great thing.

"I'm sorry, Hunter. Can I make it up to you?"

"Mmmm, maybe. Let's see what I can find to play with that might cheer me up." His fingers danced up the skin of my thigh until he encountered my panties. "Hmm, these can go."

After a little maneuvering, he got them down my legs, and they disappeared into his pocket. I had a feeling that I wouldn't be seeing those again for a while.

"And what about this? It seems there's a soft little kitty cat here. Let's see if I can make her purr."

I would have made a snarky comment about him nicknaming my pussy, but then he did something with his fingers that actually did make me purr. Or at least the moan I let out sounded like one.

"Hunter, we can't do this here. What if someone comes in?"

His mouth was working against my ear, and I lost all sense of time and place when his tongue caressed the lobe.

"It won't take long, sweetheart. I only want a few minutes."

He shifted around, and in the dim closet, I saw that he had a condom.

Oh my God. Were we really doing this?

Then he pulled his cock out and stroked the full length, and I didn't give a shit anymore. My mouth watered at the sight. I knelt in front of him, so I could take a mouthful of that beautiful part of him that brought me so much pleasure.

"Fuck, yes. That feels amazing, sweetheart." He wrapped my hair around his hand so he could better direct me. I moaned at the subtle tug of his hand. When

I looked up at him, his eyes were focused on my lips wrapped around him.

"So. Fucking. Hot." He ground out the words, completely entranced by the sight of my lips working over the swollen head of his dick. But before long, he tugged slightly, pulling me back off.

I let him go reluctantly, licking the head before placing a soft kiss on the tip. Hunter's eyes glittered with barely concealed hunger as he rolled the condom on, and then he lifted me in his arms. Bracing us against the closed door, he rotated his hips and his cock slid through my wetness. My head fell back against the door with a loud thud. He pulled back out.

"Hunter, don't tease. Give it back."

He groaned and lined himself up and pushed in again slowly. We moaned together as he slid through my tightly clenching muscles until I'd taken all of him in. I shuddered and wrapped my legs around his waist as he pulled back and slammed home again. He set a punishing rhythm that had us both panting and groaning as our shared climax raced just out of reach.

Then he moved slightly, and his next thrust hit something inside of me that made me cry out. Hunter covered my mouth with his, sucking my screams down as I came violently, shaking and scratching at his back. It was like breaking into a million pieces and being fused back together again simultaneously. Everything was heat and light and sensation, and I didn't want it to ever end.

Hunter paused and shuddered in my arms, thrusting hard one last time as he lost his fight and came with me. We stayed like that, shaking and clenching against each other, until finally, he turned his head to the side.

"Jesus, Bailey. You're going to kill me, woman."

I chuckled and the motion made me clench again, drawing gasps from us both. Hunter pulled out gently and got to work restoring his clothes, while I tried to smooth my hair. It was probably no use since there was a certain look about "just fucked hair" that no amount of tidying could hide, but I gave it a shot anyway.

"I can't believe we just humped like rabbits in the supply closet. What the hell has gotten into me?"

Hunter smiled. "Do you really want me to answer that?"

I held up a finger. "Not a word. We are going to walk out of here and avoid each other for the rest of the day. We're lucky we didn't get caught!"

He didn't say anything else, but I could feel his amusement as I opened the door slowly and stuck my head out. When I saw that the hallway was clear, I stepped out and walked back to my desk. I didn't look back or wait for Hunter.

Hunter

I stepped out into the hallway, watching the seductive sway of Bailey's hips as she trotted back toward her desk. Damn, she was so incredibly sexy. How the hell had I lasted being just friends with her this long? I was surprised I hadn't broken down and told her how I really felt before now, but I was glad I'd waited. She needed to trust me, and if her reaction that morning was any indication, she still wasn't all the way there yet.

Judging by how she was burning rubber to get away from me, maybe she wasn't very happy with me right now either. She'd wanted me all right, but knowing Bay, she was worried about how things would look.

She wasn't happy about us taking this kind of risk at work, and I could understand that. These sorts of things always seemed to be more risky for women, the gossip mill being the way it was. Men in the office could hit on anything in a skirt and talk about their multiple girl-friends, and no one said anything. But women got a bad rep. I would never want Bailey to be the subject of gossip. She hated that sort of thing. Just like she hated breaking the rules.

Yeah, I was going to be in for it tonight. I smiled.

Bailey punishing me later sounded pretty good in my book.

I turned in the opposite direction to go back to my floor, and then stopped short at the sight of Mr. Dent's receding figure walking away. Oh, shit. I glanced behind me, but the hallway was already clear. Bailey was already back at her desk. But how long had Mr. Dent stood there watching? He'd been close enough to see Bailey coming out of the closet and to see me appear in the doorway a few seconds later.

Then a gross thought occurred to me. Had we been heard? Had that sick bastard stood outside the door and listened to me screwing Bailey?

People were starting to come back from lunch break, so I started walking to the elevators. Mr. Dent was nowhere in sight and I was glad for it. It would have taken some serious self-control not to grab the guy by the throat and demand what he'd seen, but that was the last thing I needed to do. Bailey was already having issues with her boss, and now that she knew the old guy had a thing for her, this would just add another disturbing level of weirdness.

Maybe I should just pretend I hadn't seen him? After all, I didn't actually know whether Mr. Dent had seen anything. It was entirely possible that he'd appeared in the hallway after Bailey had already gone. As the elevator doors opened and I got on, I had a sinking feeling that wasn't the case.

When I got to my desk, I noticed the message light on my phone blinking. I sat down at my desk and grabbed the receiver. When I heard Bailey's voice, my dick stirred in my pants.

Down boy. No more chasing that kitty cat until tonight.

Bailey sounded just as annoyed in the message as she had when I'd left her. So much for her cooling down after getting to her desk.

"I still cannot believe we did that. I expect you to make this up to me. So tonight, I'm coming to your place after work and we will continue our earlier conversation at a more appropriate time. And I'm going to be hungry."

I wondered what she'd meant about having a shitty day already when I'd first gone to her desk. Had her boss said something to her? Fuck. This was exactly what Bailey had been afraid of, and I'd convinced her that nothing bad would happen. She took her career seriously and she'd worked hard as an intern to get a good recommendation. I wasn't going to let some pervy bastard ruin that for her.

The thought of the video file that I had backed up on my cloud drive teased at the edge of my mind. Bailey would never want that out there. I knew that instinctively. But at the same time, maybe it didn't have to be. Sometimes just the threat of something happening was enough to scare a potential enemy.

Guys like Dent were so fucking transparent. I had met many like him in my time, especially in middle management. Assholes who were past their prime and desperate to lord their tiny bit of power over anyone they could. But assholes like Dent were also cowards, and at the first hint of a worthy foe, they would slink off with their tails between their legs. They'd never actually engage in a fair fight.

If Mr. Dent got out of line, I just needed to let him know that I had some ammunition of my own. It would mortify Bailey for anyone to ever know about that video, so I'd only do it as a last resort. But I had a bad feeling the video might be the only way to keep her safe.

12

———

Bailey

This was the day from hell.

I didn't know what had crawled up Dent's ass since yesterday, or how far it was lodged in there, but he might need an emergency removal, stat. Like, post-the-fuck haste. Because if he didn't have it taken care of, then I would likely murder him.

All day, I'd been imagining the scenarios in which I could make that happen. Apparently, stabbing was a popular theme, because I found myself eyeing pens and letter openers.

No. I liked this job. And no matter what that TV show said, orange was not the new anything. I wasn't going to jail for him. To keep from completely losing my shit, I repeated over and over again, "You will not kill your boss. You will not kill your boss. You will not kill your boss."

Oddly, that didn't make me feel any better. Counting backwards from ten hadn't helped either.

The worst of it was, I had actual *work* I needed to do. I didn't know what was behind Dent's sudden need to give me menial tasks, but I was a breath away from telling him to fuck off. I had actual project work. I was a senior intern. He didn't manage my damn workload.

Yesterday, he'd taken my time demanding project rundowns, and then when I'd tried to go into any detail, he'd constantly interrupted me. Then at the end of that meeting, he'd had the nerve to say he didn't think I'd actually been doing much of anything. Therefore, he'd be giving me a few things to do.

Over the course of the last six hours, I'd developed a deep hatred of him. And not hate like I might feed orange juice to his plant, but hate like I might run him over with my car.

So far today, he'd had me run to pick up his dry cleaning. He also had me bring coffee. And of course, not coffee from the office, or even coffee from Starbucks on the corner. No, he wanted a very specific coffee from a particular cafe six blocks away. And of course, he said I could walk, instead of suggesting I use one of the company cars or offering to reimburse me for my Uber ride.

The whole day had been shit. I should've known something was up when he came by my desk and leaned way too close. His lips had practically been on my ear. I shuddered in repulsion. He'd been giving me weird looks since the day Hunter and I had fought. Had he overheard us talking?

One second Mr. Dent was yelling at me, the next he was looking at me like he wanted to rip my clothes off with his teeth. Which of course made me think about *that* night.

Ew.

Yep, that taste in my mouth, that had to be vomit and bile.

The one saving grace of the whole damn day was that in a minute, I'd be out of here and headed for Hunter's. He'd been at an off-site client meeting all day, so he hadn't seen the horror Dent had been putting me through.

If this shit continued, it was possible I wouldn't be able to continue working here. I hated the idea of giving up my internship, especially after all the work I'd put in between last summer and now, but there was no fucking way I could deal. The guy was a grade-A creeper.

When I finished the last of my project work, I saved

it on my laptop before muttering a half-hearted, "See you tomorrow" to my desk mate, Michelle.

Michelle lifted her gaze. "Don't worry. Tomorrow can only get better. I don't know what's up with Dent, but let's hope he gets over his bullshit. You know how guys are, they get all PMSy and think they can just take it out on us."

I gave her a small smile for trying to make me feel better, but it wasn't helping. Right about now, not much would help, except falling into Hunter's arms and maybe crying for an hour. Followed quickly by cookies and cream. Because there were few things that couldn't be solved with cookies and cream.

Once home, I slipped off my shoes and grabbed an overnight bag, tossing in a couple of changes of clothes. I didn't dare leave anything at Hunter's yet, although, I had noticed that his toothbrush had suspiciously made its way into my bathroom. Nothing else. Just that.

I didn't know what to make of it. I wasn't brave enough to think I could have any space in his closet or on his countertops, but I packed enough for two days. I had a feeling I was going to need some comfort over the next couple of days if Dent's attitude continued like this.

After a quick shower, and taking care to blow-dry my hair and curl it loosely on the ends, I was ready. I couldn't help but marvel at how different things had become in just a matter of weeks.

A few weeks ago, Hunter was just my friend. One of my best pals, but still just a friend. Now, everything was different. The giddy excitement made the butterflies low in my belly flutter and dance.

I grabbed an overnight bag and then my phone, making a point to snap up my charger. I couldn't go forgetting that again.

I still couldn't believe I'd almost thrown away what we had, all because I hadn't gotten a text. *Stupid.* Granted, that little bit of pain had made the make up session in the supply closet totally worth it.

I still flushed thinking about it. We could've been caught any time. I wasn't in any way an adrenaline junkie, but there was something about Hunter. I just couldn't help wanting him.

It's because you're falling for him.

I knew that was the truth. It worried me, though. Because even though Hunter said that everything would work out, a small part of me listed all the ways this could blow up in my face.

Still though, it didn't mean I didn't want to try. Because I'd never felt like this before.

———

Hunter

The moment I heard the doorbell, I raced to open the door...Not that I'd been waiting for Bailey to arrive or anything. I tugged the door open with a smile.

"Hey beautiful." But before I could lean in to give her a kiss, I could tell something was wrong. "What happened? You okay?"

Bailey shook her head as she passed by me and let herself into the living room. "No. Everything is *not* okay. I had a shit day, and all I want to do is forget all about it. So maybe you could kiss me and tell me happy things about puppies."

"Fresh out of puppy stories, but you're in luck." I took her hand and kissed her knuckles softly before tugging her closer. My lips slid over her skin as I pulled her in, and I could feel the tension easing out of her slowly.

When I pulled back, she gave me a dreamy smile. That was more like it. I didn't like seeing her stressed or worried.

"So, I have wine chilling and dinner warming. And I have my hands ready and available for all the foot rubs and back rubs you need. Want to tell me what happened?"

"Dent happened. I don't know what it is. He's got it out for me or something. He was riding my ass all day."

I choked back a laugh that had Bailey slapping her hands over her mouth.

"Bay, God, that is so gross."

"Right? Ew. Especially after everything." She shuddered.

Still laughing, I said, "How about we go with 'being a total pain in the ass'?"

"Sure. That sort of works, but if you ask me, it's too mild a term. I prefer 'asshole with the heel of a Louboutin shoved up his ass'."

I frowned. That didn't sound good. Bailey didn't usually complain about Dent. Or any of the senior execs. "Okay, so he was being an ass. Exactly what was he doing?"

I rubbed my hands over her shoulders, gently massaging out some of the tension before working my way up to her neck. My movements belied my internal turmoil. The fucker had seen us the other day. He was going to be a fucking problem.

It would be one thing to have HR pull us in for a conversation about fraternizing, but it was another thing for pencil-dick to take out his annoyance and jealousy on Bailey.

"He had me running around doing his personal errands for starters. Dry cleaning, coffee. And he wouldn't reimburse me for the Uber. Then he called a special meeting to review my progress, but it was how he asked for the meeting that gave me the ick vibes. It was so creeptastic. He leans over my shoulder while I'm working, right? And then whispers that he wants to speak to me. But he's *right next to my ear*. I could feel his breath on me." Her whole body shook with revulsion. "God, he's such a dirt bag."

I spoke through a clenched jaw. "Did he fucking touch you?"

"No. Thank God. But he's been giving me that look. Like he keeps picturing me naked and can't wait to play whack a mole with his tiny dick again."

A bark of laughter choked out of me. "Jesus, Bailey."

She shrugged. "It's true. That's the look. Like he's totally picturing me naked, or worse, picturing undressing me with those pudgy hands of his."

"We've got to go to HR."

"And tell them what? My boss is acting creepy. That he was jerking off in the office and said my name?"

"For starters."

"No. I just want to forget the whole thing ever happened."

I bit my tongue. I didn't want to have an argument with her about this, and she probably wouldn't be too thrilled to find out that I had a video of that night. Right now, all I wanted to do was make her feel good. "Okay, I hear you. What do you need?"

"I just want to be in your arms and have you kiss me. I just need to forget the whole damn day. Can you do that? Can you make me forget?"

"I think I have just the thing." I led her to the kitchen island where I had a bottle of wine on ice. She watched me silently as I uncorked it and then handed her a glass. "Here you go."

She frowned at me. "Now I love a glass of wine as much as the next girl, but when I said make me forget, I was hoping for *Hunter therapy,* not wine therapy."

My lips tipped up in a smirk. "Don't worry, sweetheart, I've got exactly what you need. You drink your wine. I'll take care of the rest."

I had been planning to wait until after dinner. First, I wanted to do the romance thing with her. We'd done the friends thing and the blazing hot sex thing, but I wanted to give her romance. I knew if I touched her, we wouldn't get to dinner for...a while.

I had plans to christen every flat surface in my apartment, but I could give her an appetizer now. A little something to take the edge off. I wanted her so bad that my hands were shaking. And as an added bonus, it would help her forget her shitty day.

I stepped behind her, wrapping my hands around

her slim waist, and then kissed her neck. The moment my lips met her skin, she sighed into the caress, and even more tension rolled away. I gently slid the strands of blond hair over her shoulder as I nipped her neck.

While my lips were busy, my hands cupped her breasts and Bailey moaned.

"Hunter."

"Sssh. I'm making you forget, remember?"

"Yes, I prefer this method much better."

I smiled to myself as I kissed along the column of her neck, followed her spine all the way down, and finally sank to my knees behind her. When I smoothed my hands up her thighs, she shivered. She was so damn soft everywhere.

Gently, I slipped one heel off, then the other, until her feet were firmly planted on the ground. With firm strokes, I massaged her feet, then her calves, and worked my way up, stopping only to kiss, lick, and suck along the way. By the time I reached the back of her thighs, Bailey was shaking.

"Hunter. Please."

"Hmm? Please what, sweetheart?"

"I'm begging you to stop torturing me. I just need to—"

"Come?" I offered helpfully.

She nodded adamantly. "Yes, that'll help me forget everything."

"Well, I feel like true forgetfulness and loss of brain function only happens on the second or third time around. So we've got a while to go yet."

Under her breath, she muttered, "Hunter Richards. If you don't bring your dick over here, I'm going to do something very, very bad."

I chuckled. "Do you promise?"

Bailey groaned as she wiggled in my grasp. "This is not a joke, Hunter."

"No. It's not. My girl asked me to help her forget. And now she's trying to direct the show. How do you think that's gonna go?"

"With a spanking?" she asked with a low whisper.

Was it me, or did Bailey really, really want a spanking? "Oh, we'll get to that. But right now I want to taste you. Then we can talk about all the spankings you might deserve."

"Hunter, do you want me to beg? I'm totally not above begging."

I chuckled as I kissed her inner thigh. "I will not be dissuaded from my task. Now open your legs wider and let me take care of you."

With every kiss and flick of my tongue over her skin, Bailey shuddered. She put her glass of wine down and laid herself across the island, her hands clenching the other side for purchase. Perfect. She was wide open to me, and ready for whatever I might bring.

I teased my thumb over the seam of the lace thong barely covering her sex. God, she was so wet. She'd already soaked it through.

Instinctively, I knew exactly where her clit was and I pressed gently, sending her into a low moan and restless wiggle of her hips. Hooking my thumbs into her underwear, I tugged the fabric aside, and took a small taste with the tip of my tongue. So goddamned sweet. Fucking heaven.

"Oh, God. More please." Bailey made this low keening sound at the back of her throat, and my dick was steel.

I didn't need her to beg. I'd been dying for a taste of her all day. I should have been there to help. *You can help her now. You can give her the most mind-blowing orgasm she's ever had.* Our previous times together were going to be tough to beat, but I was going to give it a try.

With long laps of my tongue, I licked over her, pausing only to slide my tongue into her sex and fuck her gently. When her body tried to grip me and keep me inside, I retreated, giving her the tease, a hint of what she wanted.

Bailey rotated her hips, trying to get my tongue

directly over her clit so that she could ride me to orgasm, but I wasn't letting that happen. With a frustrated growl, she started to close her thighs, and I reached up and gave her one sharp smack on her bare ass.

She stilled, then moaned low and hungry. I couldn't help a grin. I liked her response to me. I wanted to drive her crazy. I wanted her so insanely, I would do anything just for a taste of what we had. I wanted to give it to her, give her everything she needed, and then some. I wanted to light her world on fire.

Losing control of myself, I tucked both hands into the elastic at her waistband, and then snapped my wrists. The panties fell away quickly, and Bailey swore low under her breath.

"You owe me a new pair."

"Put that on my tab."

I grabbed her ass, holding it, squeezing it, loving the weight of her flesh. In between laps at her satin-soft, pale pink lips, I took little nips out of her ass, making her squeak and then moan, as I kissed away the tiny hurt.

Her first orgasm came quick. I canted her hips up and planted my lips directly over her clit, sucking fiercely, determined to make her fly. The moment I felt her body quake, I slid my tongue deep into her pussy.

But when the quaking subsided and her legs started to sag, I didn't ease up. I kept lapping at her, avoiding direct stimulation to her clit, but still driving her mad. I could tell when she was climbing back up to the top of the mountain again by the way she gasped my name, all breathless and needy.

Fuck, I loved that sound.

Just when she was nearing that peak again, shaking, begging me to just let her come already, I tried something new. After I licked her clit with the tip of my tongue, I ran over her slit, fucking her gently again. But this time, I let my tongue continue along the trail and over that stretch of skin between her pussy and her ass.

And then I ran my tongue over the hidden pucker.

Bailey jumped, but I held her firmly in position and did it again. I circled the pucker gently before probing with the tip of my tongue. The moment my tongue pressed over the bundle of nerve endings again, I rubbed my thumb over her clit, and Bailey screamed my name, the sound reverberating and echoing off of the walls.

With a grin, I placed a kiss on one of her cheeks before slowly standing behind her. I grabbed a condom out of my wallet and made quick work of my clothes and the latex. Leaning over Bailey, I smiled into her hair. "How's your memory now?"

"I don't think I remember my own name."

"Hunter Richards at your service. I aim to please." I lined up my dick to her heat, and slid home.

Bailey moaned deep. As for me, shit, I could barely think. Her body was still having remnant tremors from her last orgasm and squeezing me tight.

What was it about her? I'd had a plan. I was going to fuck her slowly. I was. Except the way she squeezed me and milked my cock, that wasn't just the tremors from before. She was doing it on purpose. She was trying to make me lose control.

"Bailey," I gritted out. "I want another orgasm from you before I come."

"Okay. Don't hold back. You come, and I'll come. I swear it."

"Jesus. *Fuck*." How had I gotten so lucky? In truth, I couldn't stop myself when she was squeezing around me. I knew I wouldn't last long. I tried to hold back, tried to slide deep and take my time. But with Bailey pushing back against me, chanting my name and gently squeezing me, there was no hope. My only chance was to make her come with me.

I reached my hand around her waist, sliding my fingers between her legs, and found her clit again.

She cried out, "Oh my God. Hunter, it's too much. I don't think I can—" And then she was flying. Again.

I didn't let up on that bundle of nerves. I kept circling and stroking as I hit her deep. Her pussy grabbed onto my dick and didn't let go, but I kept retreating, groaning in pure ecstasy while she milked me.

With her in front of me, bent over, clasping onto the island, moaning, "Yes, yes, oh God, yes. Right there," I lost all control and erupted.

I could only muster the energy to kiss the nape of her neck. "So let me ask again, how was your day, baby?"

Bailey chuckled. "It was bloody fantastic. Matter of fact, I want to do that again."

13

———

Bailey

I rolled over and smiled at the sight of Hunter asleep next to me. He looked so young like this, with the gentle, relaxed expression of someone who was completely at peace, his trademark smirk nowhere to be found. I felt like such a girl watching him sleep, but it was impossible not to want to cuddle him right now.

Was there anything sexier in the world than the sight of a handsome man in slumber with wild hair? I couldn't think of anything.

It was too bad it wasn't the weekend so we could stay just like this a while longer. I frowned thinking of what my day was going to be like. If the way that Dent had been yesterday was any indication, maybe I should just call in sick.

What the hell was up with him, anyway? He'd always been weird, but at least he'd kept it semi-professional. Now that I had some distance from the situation, I didn't think I'd been overreacting yesterday at all. All I had to do was remember his hot breath on my neck to know I wasn't being overly sensitive. In what universe did you get that close to an employee? There was no way he didn't know that he was making me uncomfortable, so why would he do that? What did he expect to happen?

Suddenly, I had a thought that made me want to barf and cry at the same time. Had Mr. Dent seen me that day? I'd assumed that he'd been too engrossed in his... activities to notice me fleeing the scene, but maybe over the past week he'd remembered something and realized that I'd heard him saying my name. Did he think that I was flattered by it?

Did he think that I would welcome his attention?

Gross. I winced thinking how awkward today was going to be if that was true. Hopefully, he wouldn't come right out and mention the Masturbation Moment directly. If I had my way, we could just ignore the entire thing. Maybe work could go back to normal, the way it was when my boss had been just slightly gross instead of completely gross.

The things I put up with for college credit.

"Hey, what are you doing up so early?" Hunter's voice infiltrated my thoughts right before his arm reached over and dragged me closer.

I laughed softly when he tucked me right against him and buried his face in the back of my neck. I was glad there was no awkwardness between us. Sometimes, even when people thought they could transition from friends to lovers, it didn't work out that way. I'd been worried that maybe Hunter would be annoyed to wake up to me, or quick to try to push me out the door. But he only seemed annoyed that I wasn't closer to him.

I sighed contentedly. It was hell trying to protect your heart from a guy as sweet as Hunter. He made it damn near impossible not to fall head over heels for him, even though I knew it was smart to guard my heart.

"I woke up thinking about what a crap storm it's going to be at work today."

Immediately, his arm tightened around my waist. "You're still thinking about Dent giving you shit?"

"Yeah. And then I realized there's probably a reason he's doing this now."

Hunter sat up so suddenly it startled me. "A reason? What reason?"

I gathered the sheet that he'd yanked off my body to my chest. "Well, yes. Clearly he's remembered something from that night. You know… Anyway, he must have realized that I saw him. I guess this is his strange way of hitting on me."

Hunter relaxed slightly. "Oh, right. When you caught him rubbing one out and screaming your name."

I peered at him. Hunter was adorable in the morning, but it was clear that he wasn't running on all cylinders yet.

"Yes. What other day would I be talking about?"

"Nothing. I'm not really awake yet." Hunter rubbed his eyes and then climbed out of bed, unconcerned that he was completely naked.

I bit my lip, watching all his muscles flexing as he stretched his arms overhead. Had I really rubbed my hands and tongue all over that fine specimen last night? Hell yeah, I had. I grinned. Maybe I wasn't running on all cylinders yet either, because otherwise I'd be touching him right now, instead of thinking about work.

"I don't want you to worry about anything, baby. It's all going to work out." Hunter leaned over and pressed a soft kiss to my forehead. His eyes darkened slightly when I lost my grip on the sheet and my breasts popped into view.

"In fact, I think maybe I need to take your mind off things again. It's the least I can do for my best friend, right?"

I whimpered when his big hands cupped my breasts. He stroked them softly before rubbing his thumbs right over the sensitive tips. My mouth fell open at the sharp sensation.

"We really shouldn't. We'll be late for work." My inner voice was screaming at me not to remind him about work, but to allow his magic fingers to continue their exploration of my aching breasts.

"No, we won't be late," Hunter crooned, talking directly to my chest. His tongue darted out, taking a gentle lick of my right nipple. "It won't take but a minute."

"A minute, hmmm? I think we can spare a minute."

I sighed as he climbed over me. All thoughts of horrible bosses were quickly obliterated by a handsome man with a very talented tongue.

And it definitely took more than a minute.

———

Hunter

A few hours later, I hung up the phone and immediately logged out of my computer. We'd managed to get to work only ten minutes late, despite my every attempt to keep Bailey longer. I'd been slammed with work ever since I arrived. My fingers tightened into a fist. The universe was working against me today; since it seemed that everything in the world was conspiring to keep me away from Bailey.

She'd seemed in pretty good spirits when she got off the elevator at her floor this morning. Not for the first time, I cursed the gossip mill, because I'd wanted nothing more than to pull her in for one last kiss before I got my day started. But I couldn't do that, at least not where anyone could see us. So I'd settled for a wink right before the elevator doors closed.

Then I'd immediately gotten on the phone with my buddy Brent in the IT department. Everything Bailey had told me the night before was exactly what I'd feared would happen. I didn't need to let this play out to know exactly where it was going. Once Dent realized that Bailey wouldn't give him what he wanted, he would threaten her job. The sad part was, the jerk knew that upper management would believe him over an intern.

Bailey had no leverage in this situation. Or at least, she wouldn't have had any if I hadn't kept the video.

Men like Dent were bullies, and they only understood strength. I had sent Brent the link to where I'd saved the video on my cloud drive. We were going to send the first thirty seconds of the video out. It would be just enough to warn Dent that someone had the power to crush him, and also put the management on notice that the guy was a scumbag who jerked off when he claimed he was working late. Dent wouldn't dare badmouth Bailey once he knew a video existed proving his obsession with her.

It was the ultimate power play. Now I just had to warn Bailey, since we'd planned for it to go out right before the workday ended. I would grab Bailey so we could leave early. There was no way to predict how Dentface would react, and I didn't want her in the line of fire.

I decided to sneak downstairs before anyone else decided they urgently needed my help, and see if I could take her for lunch. I poked my head into my boss's office.

"Hey, Stephen. I'm going to take lunch early. Text me if anything urgent comes up."

My boss narrowed his eyes slightly. "Are you okay? You've been in a mood all morning."

Damn. I thought I'd done a decent job of hiding my annoyance.

"I'm good. Just getting slammed this morning."

Stephen nodded slowly. "Cool. Just don't forget we have a planning meeting later today."

"Of course, I didn't forget," I lied. Shit, my plan to get Bailey out of here early might not work. I really needed to get down there and see her. Once I explained everything, she might decide to just plead sick and leave early on her own.

As I walked through the maze of cubicles on my floor, I saw I wasn't the only one who'd gotten the idea to leave a little early. I punched the button for the elevator and when the doors opened, the last person I wanted to see stepped out.

"Richards. I was just coming to see your boss."

I almost cracked a tooth clenching my jaw so hard. "Mr. Dent. Stephen is in his office."

Dent grinned. "I bet I know where you're going. But she's not at her desk. Hasn't been at her desk all day. Maybe you should check the supply closet."

Don't punch him in the face. Don't punch him in the face.

I stepped into the elevator. "I don't know what you're talking about."

Dent snorted. "Sure you don't."

As the elevator doors slid closed, my phone vibrated

in my pocket. I pulled it out, grateful for the distraction from my temptation to get off the elevator and beat some ass. But when I saw the text message sent from the company server, my heart leapt into my throat. Then I clicked on it, and my heart dropped all the way back to my stomach.

"Oh, fuck no." I hit the button for Bailey's floor several times and sent up a silent prayer that I could get to her before she saw the message.

14

———

Bailey

I was determined to have a good day. All I had to do was make it through without seeing Mr. Dent. Hell, I would settle for a whole hour without seeing him. I could do this.

I'd definitely had the right kind of wake-up call that morning. So a good day was imminent, right? Two orgasms was definitely the right way to start the morning.

So far, I'd managed to dodge Dent and his nonsense. Even though I'd cheated a little and gone the complete avoidance route.

As soon as we'd arrived at the office, I'd grabbed my

laptop and hidden out in the smaller conference room at the end of my floor. I'd used the morning to make most of my calls, and then had some uninterrupted work time. I hadn't been that productive in weeks.

With every email I sent to the team I was working with, I cc'ed Dent, so he'd at least know I was in the building and working. He just wouldn't be able to find me by going to my desk.

Cheater.

I stretched before diving into the work for Alta Vista, and noticed Karen from accounting walking by the conference room and staring. I waved with a smile and Karen scuttled off. What the hell was that about?

But that wasn't the only time someone walked by. There was a steady stream of folks after that, which was unusual, because no one had this conference room booked all day. To make it all stranger, no one ever took the stairs to the fifth floor, so the steady stream of folks meant people were there just to check the conference room. Maybe someone wanted to use it?

Was it so outrageous that I needed to get some work done and I couldn't be bothered to deal with Dent's personal tasks today? Maybe he was looking for me and on the warpath.

Couldn't be. He would have found me on the company's instant messenger app if he needed me. I finished up with Alta Vista quickly enough and moved on to Wendell. I was flying today. If this kept up, I'd be all caught up and a little ahead of schedule.

I ran back to my desk for the notes Hunter had given me on the Wendell project. Michelle was on a call, so I waved silently.

Her response was the same as Karen's.

I cocked my head and mouthed, "*What's up?*"

Michelle shook her head and scribbled quickly on a notepad. *You haven't seen?*

Seen what? I shook my head.

Michelle scribbled again. *Where have you been all morning? I'll come find you when I'm done with this call.*

Small conference room, I scribbled back.

Okay. Stay there.

What the hell was going on? I nodded, then quickly sent a text to Hunter before stopping off at the bathroom. I saw I had a text from an unknown number and quickly deleted it. I'd made the mistake of opening a weird text once which had given my phone a virus.

Bailey: Do you know what's going on? Feels like everyone is staring at me. Did people see us come in together?

I expected a text back immediately, but there was

nothing. After I was done in the bathroom, I washed my hands and tugged open the door to the bathroom, unfortunately running into the one person I'd been trying to avoid all day. *Dent.*

"You. You fucking did this."

Adrenaline spiked my blood and I blinked rapidly. "Mr. Dent. What did I do this time?" I had no idea what I'd done to piss him off. He hadn't even seen me all day. Not to mention, I'd been including him on all my work emails. So what was his problem?

He used his bigger body to crowd me and I backed up until I hit the wall.

"You think you're going to fucking ruin me? You're nothing. You're an intern. I will see you fired for this."

Fear quickly chased the adrenaline, and all my internal censors screamed GTFO. *Get the fuck out, Bailey. Run for the hills.*

We were in the middle of the hallway, for the love of God. He couldn't really hurt me, could he?

"I really don't know what you're talking about." I ducked out from under his arm and tried to walk down the hallway, but he followed.

"You really expect me to believe that? You think you can ruin my career?"

Clearly something had happened, but I didn't have a clue as to what. Was that what Michelle had been trying to tell me? I quickened my pace. If I could just get down to the main hallway, someone would see me. Somebody would help me. If not, I would just walk straight to HR. That seemed like a really good plan right about now.

"Mr. Dent, I assure you I don't know what in the world—"

"You're out of your goddamned mind if you think I'm going to lie down while you ruin me."

When he grabbed the front of my blouse, my mind whirled. *Holy shit.* How the hell was I going to get out of this one?

———

Hunter

What the hell had Brent done? *You did this. You fucked that shit right up.*

Fuck. I had to get to Bailey. Brent was only supposed to play the first thirty seconds of that video. Instead, he'd blasted the whole damn thing, *including* the part where Dent called out Bailey's name. It had gone out over the company's text server. So every single person who worked at Bold Horizons got that video sent to their phone.

I had to find Bailey. She was going to kill me. *Holy*

fuck. Saying she'd be humiliated didn't even scratch the surface. I needed to get to her before anyone else told her what the hell was going on.

I could almost be guaranteed that she wouldn't have gotten the message herself. For starters, she probably didn't charge her phone last night. Secondly, it would've come from an undisclosed number, and she probably wouldn't open it. Not after what happened the last time.

She'd gotten a virus and managed to infect the whole company's text server as well. So now, if her text alert didn't come from a name in her contacts, she didn't open it. Plus, she didn't always check her texts right away.

That meant I probably still had some time. Sweat poured from my brow as I ran to Bailey's desk, but she wasn't there. I glanced at Michelle, who was on the phone, and wrote her a quick Post-it note. *Have you seen Bailey?*

She scribbled back. *She's in the small conference room. I wanted to warn her about the text before she sees it.*

I nodded. *That's what I'm trying to warn her about.*

Michelle wrote back quickly. *You better hurry. Because everyone's seen it and Dent is on the warpath.*

Fuck. What was that asshole going to do to her?

I knew I'd fucked up. What I should've done was gone straight to HR, disclosed the relationship, and dealt with whatever ramifications there were. But oh no, I'd wanted to teach Dent a lesson for going after Bailey. And now that shit was backfiring big time.

I ran past the small conference room, but she wasn't there. Where the fuck was she? *Okay. Think. Think! Where would Bailey go?* Maybe she went to get coffee?

I needed to be on the offensive, to get in front of this. I sent a quick text to Stephen and outlined the problem.

Me: Not sure if you've seen the video yet but I think Dent is going to go after Bailey. Given the workload, we need to make sure she stays on the team.

The response was immediate.

Stephen: I agree. What the hell was with that video? That's just...

Me: I'll explain everything later over drinks. Right now, I need help managing the Dent situation.

Stephen: You mean how you and Bailey are seeing each other?

Oh shit. He knew?

Me: I guess I should've said something before.

Stephen: None of my business as long as you're both happy. She's not your subordinate. But do me a solid and let HR know you already disclosed to me so there's no hint of impropriety. In the meantime, I'd get Bailey out of the office.

Me: That's not a bad idea. Now if only I can find her.

I tucked my phone back in my pocket and then turned left. What I saw had my blood running cold. Dent had Bailey cornered in the hallway, pressed up against the glass. He was in her face, screaming at her about how he was going to ruin her career.

I didn't even think. Logic was not in the equation. All I could think about was saving Bailey. When I reached them, I grabbed Dent by the back of the collar and spun him around.

"If I were you I would get your fucking hands off my girlfriend."

Dent's face was a mask of blotchy red patches. His eyes bugged wide, and his thin lips contorted into a snarl.

"Oh, of course the boyfriend comes to save the day. You think I didn't know you were fucking her in the supply closet? The both of you are canned. I'm going to see to it."

I placed myself in between Dent and Bailey. I didn't even look at Bailey when I said, "Baby, I need you to walk down to HR, and do not move until I come get you."

"Hunter, what's going on?"

"Just trust me, Bay. Do it now."

But she didn't move quickly enough and Dent lunged. I really had no choice. Also, it felt fucking incredible to let loose a punch. To be honest, there was no way it was going to be a fair fight. I practiced Muay Thai three days a week. Dent was middle-aged, balding, pudgy, and hadn't seen the inside of a gym in several years, if ever. It was no match, but I gave zero fucks. That asshole had gone after my woman.

My fist connected with Dent's nose, and blood followed soon after. Dent stumbled back, and held his nose, screeching. But instead of seeing he was beaten, he lunged after Bailey again.

I had no choice. I backed him up against the wall and let loose another round of hits. "Stay put, you asshole."

Behind me, Bailey screeched. "Hunter, Stop it. What is going on?"

When Dent sagged against the wall, I turned until my gaze met hers. "A video of Dent calling out your name went out on the company's servers about thirty minutes ago. Everyone's seen it."

The color drained from her face, and she sagged back against the wall. "So everyone heard?"

I locked my jaw and nodded.

"But how did anyone see it? I didn't even know that I'd taken a video."

I was spared from answering, because I saw the moment realization dawned.

"Baby, I'm so sorry—"

She wasn't listening. Placing her hand along the wall for support, she stumbled down the hall towards HR.

15

———

Bailey

I couldn't feel a thing by the time I made it home. I was so numb after what had happened that I thought I might not feel anything ever again.

Dent's attack had been bad enough, with the way he'd come after me. He'd really wanted to hurt me. Every few minutes or so my hands would start to shake again, and I'd curl them up into fists so that I didn't scream or cry. What did I do to ask for any of this?

And then there was Hunter. The video everyone was busy laughing at, he'd been the one who had it. So how had it gotten out? Had he blasted it on purpose? Why would he do that? And I had thought I was falling in love.

No. You were falling in lust. Just because the guy's good in bed doesn't make him a great guy.

And I knew that. Despite everything that had happened today, there was still a part of me that wanted to believe in him, wanted to believe that he wouldn't intentionally hurt me. It had to be a mistake.

On top of everything else, I had to figure out what I was going to do about my job. Despite what Sally in HR said, I knew my job was probably in jeopardy. There was no way I could continue to work there. They'd heard what Dent was saying. They'd seen what he was doing. They'd heard my name. That was next-level horrifying.

Like, The Exorcist combined with that chick from The Ring and married to Freddy horrifying. Would I ever be able to look any of them in the eye again?

You didn't do anything wrong. But that wouldn't matter to a lot of people. On the other hand, I wasn't willing to throw away the year and some change I'd put into working at Bold Horizons. I had a shot at a guaranteed job after graduation. How many incoming college seniors could say that? But could I be brave enough to go back to the office? Brave enough to walk by Dent's office?

Not that he would be there, of course. Security had finally come to collect him. I'd been separated from him while his exit interview was conducted. After that, the police were called. Which was just another level of humiliation. They'd been talking to Hunter when I'd eventually left the office.

My heart had squeezed, and I'd wanted to run to him. But I hadn't. There would be no comfort there.

There was a knock at my door, and I deliberately ignored it, burrowing deeper under my comforter with my Oreos.

"Bailey, I know you're in there. Please open the door."

Hunter? *Seriously*? He thought I was going to open the door to him? I stayed quiet. Maybe he'd just go away. I wasn't ready to talk to him yet.

"Bay, I know I fucked up. I am *so* sorry. I was jealous and overprotective and wanted Dent gone. I didn't want him bothering you so I took the irritated boyfriend approach instead of the smart one. And I'm really sorry about that. That video was supposed to stop at thirty seconds."

Tears welled in my eyes and I called out. "Why would you put that out there?"

"Fuck. I know I'm sorry isn't enough. I love you. I would never intentionally hurt you."

"You what?" There it was again, that squeezing of my heart muscle. It was hardly fair. Because he was so having a John Cusack boombox moment and my heart wanted to relish it, but I was still angry, horrified, sad, and humiliated.

He kept talking. "I know I don't deserve you. But I will tell you that I love everything about you. I love that you can't take a selfie to save your damn life. I love that every time you eat Indian food your nose runs, but you still eat it as often as possible. I love that you wake up with your hair matted to your forehead because you sweat in your sleep. Do you hear me? I even love you when you're sweaty."

Mrs. Potts next door banged on the wall that separated our two apartments. "Sweetheart, if you don't want him, I'll take him off your hands."

I groaned and threw off the covers. I padded over to my door and yanked it open. "Hunter. I can't do this. Do you understand how I feel?"

He shook his head. "I will never understand how you feel. You were blindsided. I know how scared I was. I can't imagine how afraid you were. I will make it up to you in a million different ways if I can. Please don't give up on me."

"Why did you do this? Did you want to prove that you had the bigger dick?"

Classic Hunter, his lips twitched when I said that. Mine almost did too. It was a reflex with us.

"No. I didn't want to prove that I had the bigger dick.

Although, c'mon, it's obvious. But he saw us coming out of the supply closet."

My eyes rounded. "What? Why didn't you say something?"

"You were already skittish and I didn't want you freaking out again. Besides, at most, he saw us leave the supply closet at the same time. For all he knew, we were in there grabbing supplies. We weren't loud."

I flushed as I remembered why we hadn't been that loud. My mouth had been otherwise occupied. Either with Hunter's dick in my mouth, or his hand or lips encapsulating my moans. "But he saw us walk out together?"

"Yeah. He didn't look thrilled about it. But I didn't think there was much he could do. And he had nothing to go on. But then you told me the shit he'd put you through and I just reacted."

"I had no idea he saw us."

"The other night, you were so upset. I just wanted to kick his ass. Your boss being a dick is par for the course. But all that stuff about him standing too close and undressing you with his eyes worried me. I don't know what he heard in the supply closet, but I knew I had to do something." He held up his hands. "I did the wrong thing. But I was only trying to protect you."

"Hunter, I'm about to be fired."

"No, you're not. There's no way HR would do that. It's not your fault he's got you in his spank bank."

I shuddered in revulsion. "Can we not do that?"

He shrugged. "Sorry."

"Hunter, you can't run in and try and solve my problems for me."

"What would you have me do? I love you."

"I love you too, but this is important. We need to talk things out."

He grinned. "You love me?"

"Of course I do." My heart melted. I knew he was trying to help me. And he was right, Dent had been horribly inappropriate. "You did all this for me?"

He nodded. "Yes. You're it for me, Bailey. Have been since the day you first turned up. I am not letting you go. I am not walking away from this. I will bring you cookies and ice cream every day. I will send you quotes from *Sex and the City* every day. I will text you *Modern Family* gifs every day. I just want to be in your life. Even if you're too angry to take me back as your boyfriend. I can't lose Bailey, my best friend."

I searched his gaze and saw the truth in there. He wasn't going to run. He loved me. The truth of it was, I loved him too. "Want to come in for some ice cream?"

A grin broke out over his beautiful face. He pulled me close as he slid his lips over mine. "I've got something for you that's a whole lot better than cookies and cream."

———

Hunter

Relief washed through me. She wasn't kicking me to the curb. With a tremor, I reached for her. I'd panicked earlier at the office, when I had finished giving my statement and couldn't find her. Michelle had finally found me and told me she'd headed home.

"Can I kiss you?" My voice was thick and gravelly. Fuck, I needed her to want me. To trust me again.

"You can always kiss me, Hunter."

As always, the moment she was in my arms, she melted right into me, pressing her body against mine. It was so easy to get lost in her the moment our lips met. The desire and lust took hold, overwhelming me.

The little mewling sounds she made as I backed her against the wall drove me crazy. I kicked the door shut as I attempted to devour her whole. She tasted sweet and a little like chocolate, and I couldn't get enough of her. Every lick, every moan drove me to the edge. Two hours ago, I'd been terrified that Dent would hurt her. An hour ago, I'd been afraid I'd lost her forever. Now with her in my arms, I knew I was never letting her go.

Hastily, Bailey reached for my belt, and I stopped her. "Hey," I murmured against her lips, "I'm supposed to be giving you the hottest orgasms of your life. Taking my time. After what I did…"

She kissed me softly. "You will be giving me the hottest orgasms of my life. But all I need is *you*. Not some proof of how sorry you are. I need bossy Hunter, if you don't mind."

Her eyes held a glimmer of mischief and had me harder than steel.

"Now, just what does a girl have to do to get the man she loves back?" She tugged my belt out of its buckle.

"Seems like you have an idea or two about how to do that?"

"I just might."

A deep growl rumbled in my throat when she drew my zipper down. "Bailey, I—"

She reached into my boxers and wrapped her fingers around my already stiff erection. Fuck. What had I been thinking about a minute ago? I couldn't remember. All the blood used to power my brain was now powering my dick. I gritted my jaw as my eyelids fluttered closed.

God, she felt so damn good. My cock jerked in her

hand as she pumped me. She could make me lose control without even trying.

"What was that you were saying, Hunter?"

"I-I don't remember."

She released me from the confines of my clothes and sucked in a shuddering breath. She licked her lips and I groaned.

"Fuck. Bay, if you keep looking at my dick like that, I'm going to beg you to suck it."

"You don't have to beg." Bailey sank to her knees, and my muttered curse echoed in her living room. Her tongue peeked out and she laved at the tip.

Oh, fuck. I was not long for this world. I fisted my hands in her hair. "Bailey—you are so fucking good at that."

As she worked the length of me with her hands, she teased the tip with her tongue, licking and working her way around the ridge. She settled her hands at the base of my cock before opening her lips wide and wrapping them around me.

"Bailey—Jesus." My hands tightened. I didn't want to hurt her, but—fuck me. With what restraint I could manage, I eased my hold and gently massaged her scalp.

In a choreographed dance with my hips, she drew me into her mouth, hollowing out her cheeks until the tip of my cock hit the back of her throat. My eyes nearly crossed when she relaxed her throat and drew me in further.

When she drew back, our gazes met. Slowly, she released me to the tip, before drawing me fully into her mouth again. With one hand, she cupped my balls and tested the weight of them, caressed, then squeezed just enough to get my attention.

"Shit, Bailey. I can't hold on if you do that. You feel, so—aah, fuck."

She moaned as she drew me in again. My cock twitched, and my grip tightened in her hair.

"Baby, you need to stop. I'm serious. I can't—" My hips jerked. "Control, if—"

With her middle finger, she gently stroked my perineum. The result was instantaneous, as my control snapped. With a firm grip, I held her head in place and worked my cock in and out of her mouth.

It took me a moment to realize she only had one hand on me. It took me only another second to realize what she was doing with her free hand. Oh hell, my sweet, sexy girl was stroking herself.

"Jesus, Bailey, I want to be the one who makes you come." My body stilled and I dragged in sharp, ragged breaths. "Can I make you come? Can I touch you?"

Bailey released my stiff erection and shook her head slowly. "This is for you." She teased me again with a flick of her tongue, before sucking me back into her mouth.

My release hit immediately. "Oh, shit—"

With a satisfied smirk, she licked me clean. She didn't stop the soft strokes that kept me on the edge of bliss.

With shaky hands, I dragged her up my body and kissed her. "You are a very naughty little witch, you know that?"

She smiled. "Thank you. I try."

"You're going to kill me," I whispered, as I stroked a thumb over her bottom lip. My cock twitched against her body. I wasn't done with her yet.

"At least you'll have fun on the way to meet your maker."

I met her gaze with a blatant, sexual challenge reflecting in his eyes. "Well, I have something fun for you."

"Yeah, I can feel that."

I yanked up the fabric of her T-shirt and tugged down her leggings. "I don't have any condoms, so I'm going to taste you for now."

She shook her head. "No. I want you. I'm on the pill."

I kissed her, my tongue sliding against hers, sucking on her lip and drawing it into my mouth. Gently, I turned her around. As my body melded against hers and my cock nudged her backside, I whispered into her ear, "Brace your hands against the wall."

She shivered as she did what she was told. I yanked her panties down to her knees and whispered, "You are so fucking beautiful."

"Don't forget naughty."

I chuckled. "Is that what you want, Bay?"

I gently tapped her soft flesh. She shuddered, and I could feel her slick cream coating my cock as she rocked her hips. I spanked her again.

"Hunter, please," she hissed.

"I didn't think you could get any wetter."

"God, Hunter, please. Fuck me."

"I'm happy to oblige." And then I sank home.

16

———

Bailey

One week later...

I closed the door of the Vice President's office and, after glancing around to make sure no one was in the hall, pumped my fist.

"Yes," I whispered.

I gathered myself together and then continued down the hall, not even bothering to rein in the huge smile on my face. The first day back to work after Dent's firing had been awkward as hell. Even though it wasn't my fault, I could still feel the stares from my colleagues and superiors. But I'd kept my head high and pushed forward. I'd worked hard here and done my best to be a strong contributor to the team. Now, my diligence had been rewarded.

The Vice President had just told me I had a guaranteed job offer for after graduation.

When I got back to my desk, Hunter was waiting. He pushed away from the wall and approached with his hands outspread.

"Well? What happened?"

Normally, I would have enjoyed screwing with him a little bit, but I was too excited to contain it. "I got it! They offered me a job after graduation!"

Hunter swept me off my feet and swung me around. I dropped my head on his shoulder and let out a huge sigh of relief. Now that everyone knew we were dating, we didn't need to avoid showing affection, but I was still a little leery of it; however, this was the kind of moment that begged for an exception. I had a job!

"That's not even all," I said.

Hunter put me down and grabbed my hand, dragging me behind him on the way to the elevator. Once we were inside, he turned to me. "Tell me."

I loved how excited he was for me. Anyone listening would think that my news directly impacted Hunter in some way. He was just as invested in my success as he was in his own career. It was an awesome feeling to have someone rooting for me wholeheartedly.

"Stephen said there was a spot on the marketing team waiting for me. Also, in the meantime, I get to work directly on my own client, and he'll oversee my work personally."

"That's great, Bailey."

"Yeah, it is. All those times I gave ideas to Mr. Dent and he ignored them? Well, they went through his desk after firing him and found all those proposals I submitted. Upper management was impressed."

The doors opened and we walked into the lobby of the building. I slipped my hand into his as we crossed the floor and emerged into the humid August air.

"So I guess this means that you won't be leaving after graduation, then?"

I turned to look at Hunter, surprised at his tone of voice. It had never occurred to me that he might be worried about that, but it probably should have. Hunter was older and had established himself here. What would have happened if I had gotten a job in another city after graduation? The thought of having to leave Hunter behind hurt. Sure, we could have done the long distance thing, but how often did that work out? Luckily, we didn't have to worry about it, but there was a tiny part of me that wanted to know how we would have handled it. Would Hunter care enough to follow me if I got a job somewhere else?

Don't even ask, Bailey. No good can come from that.

"What would we have done if I hadn't gotten a job here?"

I cursed silently. Apparently, I had a twisted inner voice that didn't care about stirring up trouble.

Hunter squeezed my hand as we walked. "We would have dealt with it. If I had to, I would have followed your sweet ass across the country."

"Really?" I grinned, uncaring that I probably looked ridiculous.

Hunter sported a smile that was just as cheesy, and he appeared to care even less about it. "Hell yeah, I would have followed you. Not sure if you've gotten this yet, but I'm not going anywhere, baby."

"Good. That's what I really want, Hunter. This. You and me."

He winked at me. "I know. Now let's go get some lunch."

————

Hunter

The end of the day took forever to arrive. I had a mountain of work to attend to, but my mind was on one thing only.

Bailey.

My heart flipped over in my chest remembering her excitement about the job offer. It had taken all of my acting skill to pretend to be surprised. Stephen had told me about it days ago, but asked me to keep it quiet until he got the sign off from the head of the company. It was everything I'd hoped for, having my career and Bailey. The future stretched out in front of us, and it was bright. Together, we could do anything, and now we had the opportunity. I had always thought that I had shit luck, but lately, I was doing pretty well.

Now I just had to see if my luck held.

"She didn't leave yet, right?" I whispered to Michelle when I noticed that Bailey's cubicle was empty.

Michelle just shrugged. "I don't think so. Her stuff is still here."

I walked over and saw that her purse and phone were still on her desk. She must have gotten called away really quickly if she'd left her phone. I sat in her chair to wait for her to come back. A few minutes later, the soft scent of vanilla wafted over me just before two warm hands settled over my eyes.

"Guess who?" she asked in a high-pitched, sing-song voice.

"Let me see, who smells like heaven and tastes even better?"

She snatched her hands down. "Hunter! You are terrible."

I swiveled around in her desk chair. "You mean, I'm terribly good at licking that delectable little–"

Her hands flew up again and landed over my mouth. "Don't you dare finish that sentence."

I chuckled, my lips moving behind her hand. It was so easy to rile Bailey up. I'd never tell her that I did it on purpose because she was so sexy when she was blushing.

"Are you ready to go home?" she asked.

I nodded my head. She removed her hands slowly, giving me an evil look as she did it.

"Can you behave?"

I shrugged. "Not sure. I guess you should take me home fast, just in case."

She gathered her stuff quickly and grabbed my hand. I allowed her to lead me down the hallway and to the elevators. I hit the button for my floor.

"Did you forget something?" Bailey asked in confusion, when she saw we weren't heading to the ground floor.

Once the doors opened, I strolled out without answering. Bailey followed behind me. Suddenly, I veered right, yanking her after me.

"What? Where are we going?"

"I want to show you something, now that you're moving up the corporate ladder." I pulled her into the supply closet and shut the door behind us. It was bigger than the supply closet on her floor, so we had more room to move around.

"Hunter, are you crazy?"

"Yes, I am. I'm crazy about you, Bailey. That's what I should have told you last time we were in a closet together. I love you." I kissed her softly.

Bailey smiled gently, and I marveled at how completely this woman held my heart. It had been a crazy ride, but I wouldn't have changed it for the world.

"I love you too, Hunter. We never have to worry about things getting boring between us, huh? But maybe this isn't a good idea. We don't have a good history of fooling around at work."

I knelt before her and pushed her skirt up her thighs. "I figured we could use a do-over, and plus, I wanted to congratulate you on your job offer. But I could take you out for a drink if you prefer."

Bailey's head fell back against the door, as my hands walked up her thighs and my lips followed. "No thank you. This is way better than vodka."

I agreed.

17

———

Bailey

Packing had never been my favorite thing but it had been a necessary evil in my life over the past few years. Going back and forth between my internship and school, switching dorms, it had necessitated me putting all my possessions in boxes on multiple occasions.

But how was it possible that I'd accumulated so much stuff? I looked around at all the boxes I'd already sealed and then at all the stuff I hadn't even touched yet and sighed. This was going to take a while. Luckily Hunter had come over to help.

Although he'd asked me why I had so many books. I mean, really?

I guess no guy is perfect.

"So, you're really going to do it then? You're just going to leave me all heartbroken and alone?"

I threw another pair of jeans into my suitcase, all too aware of Hunter's eyes boring a hole in my back. We'd been sitting like this for the past hour, with me calmly packing my things while he halfheartedly helped and sent me those mournful looks.

"Are you sure you don't just want to move in with me?"

It was a struggle to keep my lips from curling up into a smile. This had to be the tenth time he'd casually suggested that I ditch my plans to live on campus for my last year of school and move all my stuff into his apartment.

Not that I wasn't tempted. Sure I'd had plenty of fantasies of waking up next to Hunter every morning and snuggling with him every night. But I didn't want to abandon Talia. She'd been planning her transfer for so long and we were both super excited to room together. I'd never been one of those girls who abandoned their friends when they got a boyfriend and I wasn't going to start now.

"That's moving a little fast, don't you think?"

"I don't think so. We've been in love for years."

I threw another pair of jeans into the suitcase. "We've only been dating since this summer, Hunter."

"My heart was yours since the moment we met."

He shrugged but I could see that it was hard for him to remain casual. My heart flipped a little every time I saw that look on his face. He loved me. Completely and truly.

I stopped messing with the clothes and turned to face him. He was always handsome but never more so than when he was like this, just hanging out with a T-shirt and sweatpants on. His hair was all over the place from when we'd been fooling around earlier and there was a smudge of my lipstick on his ear.

He looked disheveled and perfect. He looked like my Hunter, the one that no one else ever got to see. The one that I never wanted anyone else to see.

I guess he's not the only one who can be a bit jealous.

"I love you, too. You know that, right?"

He wouldn't look at me as he fiddled with his phone. "But you're still saying no, huh?"

Now that I had his attention, I climbed into his lap, taking the opportunity to rub against the bulge in his sweatpants. Never one to waste an opportunity to dry hump, he rubbed right back. Damn, we were perfect for each other.

"Talia and I have been planning this for ages. She's so excited about spending this last year together as roommates and so am I. I don't want to leave her hanging. She's my best friend."

His hand landing on my ass startled me.

"Your best friend *other* than me, you mean?" Hunter corrected.

I shrieked with laughter when his hand landed on my ass again. "Yes! Other than you. Jeez, so sensitive."

Hunter kissed my neck. "A guy has to make sure. Don't want to give my love to some heartless wench."

I pushed his hair back from his face. "This isn't what you wanted, I know. But I really think this is going to be a good thing for us. College goes by so fast that it'll be graduation before we know it. This way I'll be sure that we aren't rushing things. I want us to have the time to build a strong foundation before we take the next steps."

He sighed. "You're sexy when you're reasonable, Bay. Even if I'm really going to miss seeing this ass when I roll over in the morning."

Glad that he seemed to be taking things in stride, I kissed him quickly and then climbed to my feet. Over the last part of the summer, I'd spent pretty much every day at Hunter's place and while I'd loved it, I also didn't want to rush. We were young and I didn't want us to ruin a good thing by going too fast.

There was all the time in the world for moving in together and maybe even one day getting married.

One day at a time.

"Glad you understand. And I'm also glad you're here to help because I still haven't packed the books yet."

He made a pained face. "You know, now that you mention it, things *are* moving really fast. I should probably go and not come back until you're done packing."

I crooked my finger at him. "Too late. You're not getting out of this. Plus, I need your muscles. There's no way I can lift some of these boxes."

He lifted his arm and flexed a seriously impressive bicep. "Anything for you, baby."

I shook my head at his cheesy antics. "You know, not living together has some benefits. There are certain things, certain surprises, I might want to give you that are hard to do if we saw each other all the time."

He looked skeptical. "What do you mean?"

I shrugged innocently. "Well, it'll be your birthday soon. Maybe I'll come over one night with a trench coat on. *Nothing* but a trench coat on."

His mouth fell open and his eyes darkened. I glanced down in triumph at the instant bulge in his sweatpants.

"I guess that means you'll have to give me some incentive to want to come visit."

Hunter

The woman was diabolical.

As Bailey sauntered away with a naughty smile on her face, I reached down and adjusted the tentpole in my pants. It was hard to argue when I knew she was right but it was going to be really hard to move Bailey into that damn dorm room.

A co-ed dorm at that. My back teeth were going to be ground to dust by the time she graduated imagining her surrounded by horny young men who were living conveniently close.

Not that they'd have too many opportunities to try anything. Bailey didn't know it yet, but she and her friend Talia were going to have a near constant personal bodyguard. I remember college well and I've seen the kind of shit that goes down in dorms at night. Hell, I was just going to have to get used to spending time in her dorm room.

I chuckled. Maybe this wouldn't be so bad. I was already fantasizing about all the different ways I could take Bailey in one of those narrow dorm beds.

"Oh yeah, I forgot to ask you about this." Bailey appeared at my elbow waving a computer printout.

"What is that?"

She squinted at the paper. "It's my college account. Someone paid off my last year of classes. $30,000."

I leaned closer to look at the spot her finger was pointing to. I could see all the charges for her classes for the coming semester, one deduction for a grant she'd told me about and then ...

A $30,000 deposit.

"Does your financial aid advisor have a crush on you or something?"

Bailey snorted. "My financial aid advisor is about a million years old and she missed our last appointment anyway. I doubt that. I was just checking to make sure it wasn't you."

Now I wished it had been me so I could be the awesome boyfriend who swooped in with the big gesture.

"Unfortunately it wasn't me. As much as I wish I could claim it."

Bailey folded up the paper and put it in her back pocket. "Yeah, I figured. Just wanted to make sure it wasn't a crazy, extravagant gift before I called the school and told them about their mistake. I don't want some poor intern to get canned because they accidentally applied someone else's tuition check to my account."

"I only wish I could give gifts like that. I make good money with the company but not that good."

"No kidding. I don't know anyone who has that kind of money to spare."

At the thought, I stopped. It was true, that very few people had that kind of money to give away. But I knew someone who did.

Or at least, I'd been the recipient of their "gifts" before. The same person who was randomly dumping money in my bank account could have done the same to Bailey. But why? And even more interesting how would they know she needed it?

When I'd first gotten a random deposit, I had assumed it was a mistake. The bank had assured me that the transfer had been intended for my account but for the next few months I hadn't spent a penny of it sure that it would be snatched back at some point. Then that winter there had been a problem with the pipes in my building. I'd been looking at thousands in water damage that my insurance was determined not to cover.

Then I'd gotten another deposit. Too quickly for it to be random.

I glanced over at Bailey. "You may not know someone who has thirty grand to drop on a whim but I do. Or at least, I think I do. I just have to figure out who it is."

Bailey looked confused but just kissed me on the cheek and went back to her packing. Meanwhile, my mind was racing with the possibilities. When I was a kid, I used to fantasize all the time about a long-lost rich uncle coming to claim me. Not that I thought I had a rich uncle who liked to randomly deposit money in relative's bank accounts but clearly there was someone out there who knew me. Who cared about me. And they had to be close otherwise they wouldn't know when I needed money. Or who my girlfriend was.

It should feel creepy to think of someone watching me. But it didn't. Obviously they didn't want to hurt me or they could have done that already. But someone had to be close by and paying attention to my life.

It was time I started paying attention, too.

18

Hunter

I glanced out the window next to me for the millionth time. Bailey had been back in school for a few weeks now and I'd done my best to give her some space. We'd spent a lot of time with her friend Talia on campus and I'd become the third wheel in their friendship.

Not that Talia wasn't a cool chick, but I was ready to have some one-on-one time with my girl again. Tonight would be our first solo date in what felt like forever.

"Are you ready to order?" The perky redhead who had seated me at this table reappeared at my elbow. I'm sure she was wondering why I'd been sitting here alone for so long.

"No, I'm still waiting–" Something across the street caught my eye and I lost my train of thought. A man stood in the shadows next to the bus stop and he was staring right at me. The same man that I'd seen the weekend we moved Bailey into the dorms. And again outside the office one random Friday night. There was something about that face...

Movement at my elbow startled me and I realized that I'd just left the waitress hanging. Her eyes narrowed. "Sir, are you okay?"

I pulled out my wallet and dropped a twenty dollar bill on the table. "Sorry to take up a table but I need to go."

She watched me open-mouthed as I slid out of the booth and walked quickly to the front of the restaurant. The entire time my heart was in my throat, sure that by the time I got outside the man in the shadows would have disappeared just like he did all those other times. But this time, when I cleared the door and stepped out into the crisp September air, he was still there.

It took me a minute to cross the street, dodging around a stopped cab. By the time I got there, my heart was beating so hard that I had to pause, drawing in huge gulps of air. He stood watching me, not moving, his hands tucked into the pockets of his beat-up leather jacket.

"It's you, isn't it?"

He inclined his head just once but didn't say anything else or offer any other information. Something about the curt efficiency of his response jogged my memory and I smiled.

"Steven?"

He shrugged. "I told you I'd always look after you."

"That was a long time ago. I tried to find out what happened to you but no one knew."

After a long pause, he nodded once as if making a decision. "That's because Steven doesn't exist anymore. I'm Noah now. Noah Blake."

I understood what the pause was about now. He'd created a whole new life. A whole new identity. And he was allowing me to be a part of it.

"I never did thank you all those years ago for saving me from those assholes."

He held out his hand. "Truthfully, I think we saved each other."

When our hands met, he pulled me into a quick hug and I fought down a well of emotion. If you'd asked me last week how I felt about being alone in the world, I would have told you that I'd made my peace with it. My focus was on building a new life with Bailey. Creating a new family.

But there was no way to deny the intense relief I felt

knowing that my foster brother was still out here and wanted to be a part of my life. Even though I hadn't known it, I'd had a family all along.

* * *

Bailey

Curled up on the couch, I let out a long sigh. My classes were intense this year since I was taking all the hardcore marketing classes needed to complete my degree. Tonight was a welcome reprieve from having my face buried in a textbook.

"Sorry about being so late. I really wanted to try that restaurant but I got distracted studying for my test."

Hunter hummed absently. I pulled back to glance at him. He'd been acting strangely all night. Not like he was angry at me or anything but just really distracted. Maybe something was going on at work.

"Is everything going okay at the office? Did you get a new client?"

I leaned over and grabbed another eggroll from the carton on the coffee table. Since I'd been so late, Hunter had texted me to just meet him at his place and he'd order Chinese. It may not be as fancy as going out to a restaurant but I was just as happy. Eggrolls and lo mein made me a happy girl.

Hunter blinked. "No, everything is fine. It's actually been surprisingly boring now that the gossip mill has finally stopped talking about Dent."

I rested my head on his chest. The sound of his heart beating beneath my ear was comforting. In that moment, I could imagine how things would go over the next few months. I'd finish school, Hunter would continue to be a superstar at the office and we'd be together through it all.

Things were especially perfect now that Talia was here. It was starting to feel like everything in my life was coming together. When I mentioned that to Hunter, he chuckled softly.

"What?"

He pulled me closer and kissed my forehead. "Nothing, baby. I'm just happy. I have you and I have my family. For the first time in a long time, everything is going right."

It took a moment for his words to register. Family? Even though it wasn't something we talked about often, I knew that Hunter had grown up in foster care. All the pictures in his house were of him with his friends or people at the office.

And me, of course.

"Family? What does that mean?"

Hunter winked. "Just that family really is what you make it. And someday soon, I want to take you for a little ride. There's someone I want you to meet."

———

THANK YOU FOR READING WICKED. Want to know more about the mysterious Noah Blake? Keep reading for an excerpt of his book, *Shameless*.

EXCERPT OF SHAMELESS

I am the thing that goes bump in the night. I am a liar, a protector ... a killer ... I am Noah Blake.

There is only one light in my darkness, one bright ray in the storm of my life. Lucia DeMarco. And I'll do anything for her. Anything except show her who I really am: an assassin. Well, former assassin. I don't really do that anymore ... usually.

It would be easier if she didn't call me names. Asshole, control freak ... shameless. It would also be easier if she didn't look at me with those trusting gray eyes. If I didn't dream about the perfect curve of her — Never mind all that. The point is she's digging into my world, my secrets, and it's going to get her killed.

But first, we have another more immediate concern. Lucia is going on a *date*—with someone else ...

And I'm not allowed to kill this one.

Excerpt of Shameless © May 2017 M. Malone and Nana Malone

———

Noah watched the date from the comfort of his SUV. All the while silently fuming.

What the hell did Lucia think she was doing? His team hadn't vetted the guy. They didn't know anything about him. So far, she'd broken all of the dating rules he'd given her.

For the first date, always meet your date at your designated location. And of course, she'd let this doofus pick her up for their date. As if he hadn't told her a million times to do the exact opposite.

He'd also been very clear not to get in the car with her date. So that was rule one and rule two broken right off the bat. As if he hadn't trained her on how to be careful and what to watch out for. But *oh no*, Lucia didn't listen to shit. Every time he turned around, there she was, careening headfirst into trouble.

Maybe she didn't see her date as a potential threat, but dammit she needed to be more careful. What the hell did she even know about this guy?

"What the hell kind of name is Brent anyway?"

Noah hadn't even realized that he'd spoken out loud, until the voice in his comm unit laughed. "Last I checked, Brent is a perfectly normal name. Lots of guys have it."

Noah barely restrained a growl. "Matthias, when I want your input, I'll give it to you."

There was a chuckle on the other end of the line. Noah made a mental note to give Matthias some really horrible surveillance duty for the next month. This wasn't funny. This was Lucia. They all cared about her well-being.

Maybe you more than the others.

Yeah, so what? He cared about her. And maybe it wasn't the easiest thing in the world watching her date loser after loser. But it was his job, no strike that, it was his *responsibility* to look after her. He owed Rafe that much. But how the hell was he supposed to look out for her when she kept making it so damn difficult? Lucia was obstinate, infuriating, pigheaded, and—

Beautiful.

No. She was like a little sister to him. Yet somehow his dick couldn't seem to get with that program lately. More and more frequently, some very *unsisterly* thoughts wormed their way into his consciousness.

"Matthias, give me something on this Brent guy. Aren't you supposed to be some kind of super-hacker?"

"You better believe it. But, there's nothing on him. Everything is normal. Boring. Most interesting thing about this guy is he likes adventure sports. He skydives, bungee jumps, that sort of thing. Does some triathlons. Maybe he's some kind of adrenaline junkie. But there's nothing else on him. No flags. He lives here in New York in the East Village. No roommates, rent isn't exorbitant. Works for the city. No large withdrawals of cash, good credit. As far as I can tell, he's clean. But that's just his electronic trail. Maybe you're right on this one and he's a little too clean. I mean, there's not even an online dating profile on him. To me, that's weird. Who doesn't have an online dating profile?"

Noah chuckled and then lifted his binoculars again. Lucia was laughing at something. So Brent thought he was a comedian, huh? What the hell was so damn funny? There was too much interference to use the boom mic, otherwise he'd know.

Brent reached across the table and took Lucia's hand, and Noah nearly chipped a tooth from grinding his teeth so hard. He could see Lucia's eyes go wide. Was that surprise? He hoped it was disgust.

Did she actually like this guy?

His gut clenched at the thought. Perfect, just what he needed. Lucia liking this fucking idiot.

It wasn't that she hadn't dated before. She had. Mostly in college. Most of those guys had merely needed a strong reminder to mind their Ps & Qs with her. But this guy, this guy was random—unknown. Which meant it would take more work to scare him off. But Noah was up for the challenge.

Lucia deserved to be happy, just with somebody vetted and approved. After the shit she had survived in her life? The girl needed some happy endings.

Fuck. Not happy endings.

He groaned and turned his attention back to the restaurant. Brent raised a hand and signaled their server. Shit, they were leaving. The real trick was guessing where they were going. He'd put a tracker on her phone, so if he guessed wrong, he could always follow. But what if something happened to her before he could get there?

"Matthias, turn on the listening device on her phone. I'm heading to the house in case that's where they go."

There was a beat of silence. He could almost hear Matthias's silent condemnation. "The thing is, Noah, she's not going to like that."

"The thing is, Matthias, I don't care," he muttered using the same singsong tone.

Yeah, he knew he sounded like an asshole. But this was Lucia. If she wasn't going to take care of herself, that left it to him to do it for her. They had one simple rule: He vetted all her dates. And sometimes, without her knowing, he'd scare them off. But that was really beside the point. It wasn't his fault she couldn't pick a decent guy.

He made a left turn on 10th Ave, right near the USB Theater, then he sped through Chelsea before making a left on 28th Street, heading toward Chelsea Piers. He made a right at the stop sign, turning onto her quiet street. The street was lined with lofts and new apartment high-rises, all boasting a name with Arms, or Manor.

Before she'd moved, Noah and his team researched the building's owners and the neighborhood crime rate. Everything to make sure she would be safe. Well as safe as she could be in Manhattan. It also didn't hurt that he watched her every move. And not in some creepy, stalkery way, but more like a big brother way. *Sort of ...*

Never mind that. He drove past her building and around the back to the lot he paid for specifically for these kinds of situations. Yeah, so maybe he also paid most of her rent. She thought she'd gotten extremely lucky with a rent-controlled apartment in the heart of the city. In reality, he paid most of the tab. He also paid for two parking spots. Not that Lucia had a car. But in case she ever got one, she'd have somewhere safe to park it. Somewhere right next to the damn elevator. He paid almost as much to secure that spot as he paid for the apartment. His spot was in the darkened shadows somewhere she'd never think to look. He didn't mind though, because in most scenarios, he was the thing that went bump in the night.

"Matthias, talk to me. Where are they headed?"

"They're stopping for ice cream at Benny's then he's going to take her home."

Okay, so Noah had about ten minutes. Benny's was a

local mom-and-pop ice-cream place about five blocks away. He jogged along the parking garage to the side stairs. While he'd insisted that she get a building with a doorman, there was no accounting for the additional exits and entrances into the building. Luckily, this one was exit only. Only confirmed residents had keys. Unfortunately, even your average guy could pick these locks, and he happened to be better than average.

In less than a minute, he was through the door and took the back stairway up to her apartment. She'd listened to him and employed the deadbolt. Problem for her was he had a key.

In seconds he turned off her security alarm. Well, at least there was that. Lucia had been so against it in the first place. At least she realized that a woman living alone needed *some* security. He glanced around and noted that she'd changed a few things. Was that a new pillow?

Matthias spoke into his earpiece. "You've got about five, boss. They've stopped outside the apartment. I'm going to go ahead and turn off the mic on her phone now if that's okay with you."

More judgment from the youngest member of the team. Whatever. He'd deal with that later. Now, the real question was where to wait for her.

What if she brought the guy in here?

Oh hell no. The mere idea of it had him gripping the edge of the countertop. She had better be coming in alone.

Didn't she know the first thing about dating? Damn it, this was their first date. She was supposed to make the guy twist in the wind for a bit first.

How many one-night stands have you had?

No. He was not going to think about that. It was different. That's all. Besides, Lucia was a good kid. And there was no way Nonna DeMarco would approve.

He'd give her a few minutes to run the guy off herself, and then the two of them were going to have another conversation about dating and personal safety.

She couldn't really be interested in this guy, right? He was boring. *Unlike you?* Noah grimaced. Yeah well, she didn't need to date anyone like him either. If she did, Noah would have to employ more drastic measures to keep her safe.

No. Lucia needed a nice guy, but someone more interesting than a records keeper.

Okay, if he was going to give her the chance to send Brent packing by herself, he needed to wait somewhere other than the living room. If she caught sight of Noah first, and if she was carrying that Taser he'd given her for Christmas, he might end up as fried toast. He jogged down the hallway and turned left into her bedroom, gently closing the door behind himself.

He hopped onto her bed, bouncing slightly and leaned back against the pillows. *I've always loved how girly she is*, he thought, enjoying the scent of her perfume in the room and looking around at the four-poster bed, the soft colors, and all the ruffled pillows. He also loved that when she completely lost her temper her curls went flying and her eyes snapped with anger.

It was probably why he enjoyed pissing her off so much.

Something caught his eye as he lay back against the pillows, readjusting them for his comfort. Her bottom drawer was open.

Do not open it. Leave it be. She won't appreciate — Oh fuck it.

He pulled it open and took out his phone, shining the flashlight directly inside.

"Well, well, well. What do we have here?"

Read Shameless now at malonesquared.com/shameless

ABOUT THE AUTHORS

NYT & USA Today Bestselling author **M. MALONE** lives in the Washington, D.C. metro area with her three favorite guys, her husband and their two sons. She holds a Master's degree in Business from a prestigious college that would no doubt be scandalized at how she's using her expensive education.

Independently published, her work has appeared on the New York Times and USA Today bestseller lists more than a dozen times. She's now a full-time writer and spends 99.8% of her time in her pajamas. **minx-malone.com**

USA Today Bestselling Author, **NANA MALONE**'s love of all things romance and adventure started with a tattered romantic suspense she borrowed from her cousin on a sultry summer afternoon in Ghana at a precocious thirteen. She's been in love with kick butt heroines ever since.

With her overactive imagination, and channeling her inner Buffy, it was only a matter a time before she started creating her own characters. Waiting for her chance at a job as a ninja assassin, Nana, meantime works out her drama, passion and sass with fictional characters every bit as sassy and kick butt as she thinks she is. **nanamaloneromance.net**

www.ingramcontent.com/pod-product-compliance
Lightning Source LLC
Chambersburg PA
CBHW060552190726
48283CB00003B/979